I0574295

GOOD NIGHT ROOM NINE

ISBN-13: 9781666400953 (Hardcover)

ISBN-13: 9781666401721 (Paperback)

Cover design by: Cindy Thai

Dedicated To

the strangers we meet along the way,
the ones that inspire us in passing to manufacture realms
we don't belong to but greatly admire.

Table of Contents

0

"There is so much history here, *ljubezen*," her grandfather's slow, delicate voice croaked through her cell phone's aging speaker. His accent worked through each syllable like a sculptor chipping away at a block of expensive marble. "Not all of it good, but all of it beautiful. If one day you travel through the country, you will see old buildings and even older trees. Creatures—they live there. Their family has always lived there. So, when will I see you?"

She promised they would finally meet the following day. Her eyes were sewn to the conveyor belt where eleven bags that weren't hers passed by. Pressure pushed against the back of her tired eyes.

"Oh, but not today? Mm. I do not know if I can sleep tonight, then. No more coffee today. Ah! I, eh... I printed the photo you sent. The *selfie*."

Jenny smiled and couldn't shake the red from her cheeks. She finally retrieved her checked bag, hoisted it off the track, and blew a wispy exhale. The backpack that had been tossed over her shoulder slipped half-way down her arm. "Aw, really? That's—where'd you put it? On the fridge?"

"The *fridge*," he repeated, then understood. Clarity polished his voice. "Yes. The refrigerator, next to a photo of your father." Jenny prepared for the single most ubiquitous comment of her life. When it inevitably splashed against her ears, a warmth entered her core instead of the typical cold embarrassment. "You look just like him, you know?"

"I've been told." He then asked why she wouldn't drive directly to him. After describing a chaotic morning that

7

started much too early, she added, "And I'd hate myself if I didn't explore, even if it's just for a little bit. My overinflated sense of curiosity is your fault, by the way."

She could imagine his eyes widening. "Oh, is it? How is that so?"

Ancient stories of her grandfather emerged in a rapid remembrance, how he would hike every mountain his eyes landed on and biked every trail he'd happen upon; how he'd bring home a rotating cast of women after his wife died and how his drink of choice changed week-to-week; how he left Australia because he could no longer face his son.

Jenny's father, an ex-police officer, claimed to have inherited his adventurous and careless spirit from his dad. In a low moment of his life, her father blamed the injury that left him paralyzed on the old man. The eternal desire of a son to impress his father brought his downfall; the desperation to climb higher, more dangerous heights with less equipment and under an arbitrary, self-imposed time frame. He attempted to beat a clock that never existed to appease an expectation that had never been set.

A flame stoked in her stomach, and her face flushed.

"You keep telling me how beautiful Slovenia is!" Jenny said after some contemplation. She stressed some laughter and hoped it would ease any inadvertent tension. "I had to see it for myself. Pictures on a computer can only do so much."

"Well," he eked out after some consideration. A hesitation carried his next question as though it was a pallbearer slinking along a funeral procession. "That I can understand. You're right about the beauty. But, Jenny, where will you sleep tonight?"

1

There was enough sense left in Jenny Novak's tired skull for her to feel hesitant when standing at the threshold of a visibly decaying bed-and-breakfast somewhere deep within a country she didn't belong to.

Ambling beech trees invited her down a half-paved and terribly bumpy path until the creaking inn revealed itself to her like a moth exfiltrating its cocoon. Old paint, once brilliant gem tones now dull and unimpressive, flaked from wooden panels. Time threw shingles to the overgrowth below. As derelict as the building seemed, plenty of movement churned inside. Each of its many windows contained a dull overhead lamp that illuminated each room in a sickly orange glow. Terracotta curtains accentuated the building's antiquated aesthetic.

Her tan knuckles rapped against the door, and she could see through the window an abrupt freeze from a patron indoors. Jenny heard his voice mumble something before erupting into a brief coughing fit; the truncated and bassy vibrations rattled the glass panes. She preemptively chose to wear her noise-canceling earplugs for the night.

Jenny made way for a rake-thin woman to open the door. It swung outward and forced her to teeter on the edge of the top step. She swung a quick glance behind her to check that each window of her antiquated rental car had had been rolled up. The woman greeted her in her native Slovenian, and Jenny forced the only greeting she knew.

"Australia?" the innkeeper quickly tilted her head.

"Oh, impressive. You identified my accent from one word?"

"*Y-y-yes,*" she stretched her reply, obviously lost for additional English. "Staying here?"

"I am." Jenny craned her neck to peer in. The interior of the inn had been well decorated, with much more modern furniture than she expected. Her internal biases muted for a moment. She should've readjusted her expectations after landing in the gorgeous Ljubljana, but the farther she traveled into the country, the less she was convinced comfort waited for her. "Visiting family. Just need to stay the night."

The woman peered past the furrowed canopy and into the sky. "Nightfall, very soon. One night?"

"One night."

"Okey-dokey," she stepped out of the way and gestured for Jenny to move inside. A stinging waft of old garlic clung to the air and the potent scent of dried herbs followed close behind, clawing its way into her sinuses. "One vacancy. So, you are lucky." As if borne from an autonomous reply, she colorlessly said, "My name is Sabiha. Nice to meet you. Take the chair."

Jenny turned to and admired the beautiful seats and their intricately sewn cushions. Red and gold geometry wrapped around each other before meeting in the middle to create the face of a muscular canine breed. Her hand reached out to trace the impressive design without her brain willing it to.

"Go ahead, take the chair," Sabiha demanded. The innkeeper slipped behind her squat, heavily varnished dark wood desk. Its surface reflected the same orange glow from the sconces installed in each room. A shallow bowl of hard candy rested next to a stack of papers. "One minute."

Jenny unloaded a small backpack of essentials from her left shoulder. The bag decompressed when she laid it against the polished floor. She crossed her legs and entered a patient meditation, drinking in some of the finer details of the bed-and-breakfast's interior: hyper realistic portraits of hounds, fresh flowers in long vases.

A man limped his way over and lowered himself next to her with a sustained grunt. The scent of strong coffee and parsley scored Jenny's nostrils.

"O-oh. Welcome, new guest!" The man said. "I am Romeo." His large, mittenish hand reached toward Jenny, and she accepted the stranger's gesture after a beat of hesitation. The muscles in her arms tensed once locking her hand with his; it felt like she was greeting an old carpet.

Romeo said, "I speak better English than my wife. She's educated, yes, but this is her chosen life. The countryside! I am more of a city boy." He chuckled, then doubled over in a cough that constricted his chest. She picked up the smell of stale, wet tobacco. "Apologies. You know, we used to board dogs here."

A cocked brow complimented Jenny's feigned interest. "Is that right?"

"Yes, it is right. Many, many years ago. My father bred shepherds in Turkey. He moved to Bulgaria, then Slovenia. He wished one day to be in France. To be honest," he continued while admiring the portrait of a Mastiff hanging on the wall. "The dogs? It is quite similar to boarding *people*." A wry chuckle turned into another coughing fit.

Sabiha called out something that must've equated to, *oh, leave the poor girl alone!*

Her indignant husband waved his wife away and asked, "Did I hear correctly that you have family in Slovenia?"

"Um," Jenny rolled her shoulders back and nodded. "Yeah, I do. My dad's parents."

"Let me guess. It's your first time meeting them?"

"Yep!" She shifted in her seat and tapped the cell phone hidden in her jean pockets. All her mental strength siphoned into manifesting a phone call or text from anybody—*anybody*—just to avoid the continued social interaction with a man who absolutely radiated the aura of spent coffee grounds and sweat.

"That will be a very special moment," he nodded. His focus gently settled onto his wife and her dainty movements; her quick tapping of a clunky keyboard connected to a thick, beige monitor. "Even if you do nothing together but watch television, it will be special. Something always to remember."

Jenny dried her clammy hands along the side of her jeans. A small part of her wanted to fall into old, introverted ways. After spending the last year managing a small coding team in Brisbane, she'd become more used to public speaking after presenting countless projects. The man's sentiment appeared to be genuine, so the least she could do was play along. "Yeah, you're right."

"But, why now, after all this time? Did something happen, or is he sick?" When he turned to ask this, she glimpsed past his rough, frog-like exterior and saw light behind his eyes. "I-I'm sorry. Sabiha says I speak too much."

"No, you're fine," Jenny squeezed her knees. "Um, he's not sick or anything. It's just time, you know?"

He nodded. "The best thing to realize is that it is always 'time'. Family is the most important thing. You know, Sabiha and I sacrifice very much for our boy. Long hours, no vacations. Our money becomes his money for university, clothes—maybe one day a girlfriend. Ha ha! We imagine him in a house with a gorgeous, stunning, supermodel wife and us with handsome grandchildren." Romeo leaned back into the chair that matched hers and wrapped either arm over his barrel chest. "You are not the first Australian we have. Not the first Australian we... *Have* have?"

She tentatively corrected him. "Have *had*."

His head pivoted in shame, and he leaned forward. "Once upon a time, I was very good. Well, if you have questions, any questions *whatsoever*"—he added if not just to flex his linguistic abilities—"find me down here. My wife, she is the one who cleans the rooms and makes the food."

Jenny couldn't stop her next words from seeping away from between her lips: "Then what do you do?"

"Me?" His bushy eyebrows perked. "I make world famous coffee. What a skill, eh! Speaking of... Do you want some?"

"N-no," she said with raised eyebrows. Night had fallen hard, and Jenny suffered from shocks of adrenaline every time she thought about meeting with her grandfather. The less stimulation, the better. "I appreciate the offer, but no. Definitely not. I can already tell I'm not going to sleep tonight, anyway."

"I can drink two pots and still sleep like a baby!" With one wink, Romeo lifted himself from the chair, coughed a few times, and exited from the quiet lobby into the kitchen. The sink squealed like a throat-slit hog when Romeo turned it on. Pipes clanked and banged within the walls around her, and the rushing hiss of water crescendoed before dying with a whine.

Romeo hummed a throaty, familiar tune, its resonance deep enough to carry throughout the empty lobby. Though he mangled every other note, Jenny identified the song as Australia's national anthem.

Sabiha snapped twice to conjure Jenny's attention. "Okey-dokey, room nine for you." The loop of a long brass key hung off the bend of her pointer finger. "Sorry for my husband."

Jenny tentatively slid the key from the woman's long pointer finger. "Right, thanks. May I ask a question?"

"Question? Yes, yes. Of course. What is it?"

"This little bowl here," she nodded to an apparently hand-blown glass bowl filled with pungent, bone-colored garlic cloves. Curated sprigs of parsley and dill heightened its aromatics. "Are these, like, free samples, or...?"

"N-no. No, please do not eat. This is for—for, um, eh, our *religion*." Sabiha didn't appear satisfied with her word choice but shrugged it off to keep up the momentum of their conversation. "You're hungry, then ask Romeo. I make breakfast at..." She grimaced while counting in her head. "S-s-six in the morning. Okay?"

Jenny scratched behind her ear. Since her job required her to work at home, the idea of waking up before seven nauseated her; the last time she'd done so had been to catch her flight to Ljubljana, and even then, a little voice pleaded with her not to get out of bed. With a sigh, "Sounds good."

"*Sounds good,*" Sabiha repeated, blinked, then nodded once she processed the apparent meaning. "It *is* good. Are you hungry now?" The woman pulled open a flimsy drawer and grabbed a handful of individually wrapped halva. She thrusted her hands forward. "Take, take."

"Oh! Um, thanks." A clumsy exchange occurred. When Sabiha smiled, her jaw disappeared under a pronounced overbite. Jenny pocketed the snacks while the woman grabbed for a second portion. "That's okay, thank you! I have some granola bars in my bag if I'm still hungry."

Sabiha beamed. Her wrinkled lips parted to show a set of yellow-brimmed teeth. The expression reminded Jenny of a braying horse. A gleam sparkled in the woman's eye as she said, "*Lahko noč*, room nine."

A temporary deafness pushed into Jenny's ears. She struggled to recall a response from one of her recent phone conversations with her grandfather. Sabiha's words were familiar, but she couldn't dredge up the meaning. Jenny scoured the memory of a handwritten phrase book her dad gifted to her—a relic of his one attempt to reconnect with his father.

The innkeeper stared expectantly, and her grin slowly died away.

Jenny remembered her grandfather had said this to her several times before, but never bothered to ask him what it meant. She felt embarrassed not knowing even elementary-level words from a language most of her family knew.

Sabiha lowered her voice and leaned in. Her breath smelled of tahini and rose. "This one means *'good night'*."

"Right!" Jenny's tongue hovered over the simple Slovenian phrase, terrified to mispronounce it. Tendrils of defeat reached from her heart and promulgated throughout her limb. With a hanging head, she resorted to English. "Um... Yeah. G'night to you, too."

Heat seared her cheeks, and angry butterflies crashed against her esophagus. She repeated the foreign words under her breath after snatching her bag and rushing away. "*Lahko n-noč. Lahko... Lahko noč.*"

Jenny paused at the first step of an old staircase with the desire to shout *lahko noč!* to the Slovene woman who no longer paid attention to her. Instead, Sabiha fought with the slick halva wrapper and cursed when dust exhaled from the opening.

Jenny promised herself she'd listen to an audio course during the next day's drive. *I already bought the damn thing*, she reasoned while imagining her grandfather's face after pulling up to his property and greeting him in his native language. *I just have to do it. Why haven't I done it?*

Her nostrils flared while ascending an old staircase.

2

The flight creaked and moaned with every step. Jenny tried to be quiet out of respect for the other guests. She hesitated, gulped, and toyed with placing pressure on less-worn areas as though she were Indiana Jones and the wrong placement meant death-by-boulder. By the time she reached the top of the long flight of skinny steps, she was sure she woke up everyone in the building.

Figuring they were awake anyway, Jenny fought the urge to apologize to each guest in Slovenian, just to redeem herself from her failure with Sabiha.

Classic me, she thought. *The only thing I know how to say is sorry.*

A half-day prior, she stepped off the plane and knocked into a soft-cheeked older male who seemed dressed for strict academia. He apologized to her in Slovenian, and the phrase burned hot.

"*Se opravičujem!*" All she could do was smile and nod. The words sounded like an alien language to her Western ears. As soon as he floated out of earshot, she called her grandfather.

Jenny butchered the phrase three times before he translated through a chuckle. "It means he is sorry. But, for what? Everybody makes mistakes—this, I should know."

She relegated the translation to the forefront of her mind in a green folder labeled *Necessary and/or Useful Information.*

The long hallway, suffused with dim points of copper light, appeared to stay petrified in time. Not a mote of sound traveled from within the rooms or outside of them. No clocks ticked the day away, no televisions provided background ambiance. She softened what she suddenly considered to be heavy footfall.

Nobody stuck their head out to yell at her for causing a commotion. If they did, Jenny imagined they would be old men in stained white singlets or batty women donning long floral dresses and hair curlers.

Looking down the amber-tinted corridor, there were no identifying factors that convinced her she had entered another country. The walls were made from the same wood she'd find at any local inn, the same doors plucked from some cheap manufacturer, and the same ceiling—smooth and endless—reminded her of every other hotel she'd ever stayed in.

Several portraits of dogs were crooked and dusty. She wondered if the dogs were real—if they had names, allergies, or roamed the same halls. Fresh flowers with orange hearts and white limbs slept in a ceramic vase by room five.

The corridor seemingly stretched in jest the longer she traveled through it. Jenny tuned into the eight rooms she passed before reaching hers and heard nothing behind each door. Suite ten and the unmarked suite across from it end-capped the hall with a curtained window framing the empty space between them. Exhaustion gripped her eyes, but she felt called to look out of the window.

A frigid chill strengthened the closer she came to the cold glass. Her fingers pressed against its surface before swiping to move a stiff curtain out of the way.

Beyond the portal was an expanse of woods, obfuscated by night yet touched by the caress of a watchful full moon. She squinted to make out the vein of a large stream, lifted her brow, and allowed a smile to eke on her face. If she intended to wake up at five-thirty in the morning for breakfast, she might as well take a walk and explore right after.

Jenny's typical method of decompression had always been swallowing as much fresh air as possible; her job required her to drink the same stagnant air, to feel the same irradiated glow of her dual monitors. Detouring from her agenda to wander in the Slovenian wilderness would be worth the apology she'd offer her grandfather. He was a patient man who spoke slowly and lived slower—he wouldn't mind the wait.

The few times they talked over the phone were typically one-sided conversations. He would chuckle at the things she said, even if he didn't quite know how to respond. Jenny brought him up to speed about the shows she binged or described the footage of drones soaring above her ancestral home. He held no opinions about either and casually responded with a lethargic, *"ah, is that so?"*.

The old man had removed himself from the bustle of everyday life after his son's spinal injury and instead lived in solace, away from modern technology, people, and their influence.

Jenny's dad once shared a conspiracy about his father. "He's afraid of judgment," he said after being sat upright in the living room. The television purred in low, scripted conversation as he spoke. "Has a fear of gods that don't exist. Has a fear of people, because they can't read his mind. In his head, he's a saint who gave everything to his children. If only they could, they'd see how good of a person he is, right? Listen to me: he's not a terrible man, but what did he provide me? Certainly not a role model. Someone to compare myself to, sure—but not a role model."

She could only pry so much before he inevitably shut her down to change the subject.

The presence of a shadow lumbering from beyond the window coaxed Jenny back to reality. She trained her eyes onto the lackadaisical form and watched it slink between narrow tree trunks or forage from the bushes. It had a large head and was diminutive in size. No matter how hard she squinted, she couldn't hope to identify what the animal had been.

Creatures—they live here, her grandfather told her on Halloween; she said she didn't believe in ghosts when he asked. *Their family has always lived here. Those are the ones who haunt.*

Freshly convinced the strange country hid unfathomable beasts from her, Jenny cherished the safety of being behind walls.

Jenny pulled away and wielded the ancient key in a firm death grip. The door to her room unlatched without difficulty. After one hesitant step inside, she drank in its dank interior.

The smell of old dander clung to her heels, following her wherever she moved. The cramped room contained a full-sized bed, its comforter both cold and damp to the touch. A single shoddy dresser towered directly across the bed. One chair coupled with a matching table, and the corner hosted a hovel of a bathroom.

"At least I don't have to share," she muttered.

Jenny stuck both hands in either pocket and blew a raspberry of disappointment. Halva packaging crinkled under her fingers. She very much disliked the flavor of sesame. Her first order of business was to throw away the gross snacks and make a meal out of a granola bar. The second, a natural consequence, would be unpacking toiletries and brushing crumbs from her gappy teeth.

The structure of her bathroom mirror lagged her: three, slim panels of glass each responded in different intervals of time when she rotated her face. The more time she spent staring at the tan, pill-faced and tired looking doppelgänger, the more Jenny convinced herself each panel portrayed a different version of her.

These faces watched through the reflective portals, each dwelling in an alternative realm localized within the glass. She almost believed that, if she smashed the reflective faces, another world would be waiting for her.

Afterall, Slovenia remained a mystery and Jenny had no idea of its potential. She prepared to be met by a satyr or a fairy godmother after tracing her fingers along the mirror's edge to pop it open.

Each panel opened to reveal an empty cabinet where her toiletries would be stored for the remainder of her stay. Her eyes pulled away to examine the interior of the bathroom: a shower curtain fumigated the stench of mildew, and yellow crescents painted the drain's perimeter.

No, she wasn't in Narnia. Jenny would have to be okay with her role as *Hotel Guest*.

She prepared to wind down. A freezing stream of water poured from the faucet and eventually warmed up the more she berated it.

"Come on, you piece of shit. Come on."

Sulphur wormed its way up her nostrils and superseded the ever-present rot of garlic that stained each room.

After completing all the tasks that made Jenny feel clean and comfortable, she set her eyes on the bed. The sharp twang of garlic reemerged like a venomous snake striking from tall grass. She followed an almost visible scent tail to locate a palm-sized decorative bowl sitting on the empty desk. Three cloves, each old and translucent now, were adorned with fresh garnish.

Jenny picked up one clove and rolled it between her fingers. It felt tacky, almost dry. She stared into the surface as though it were a scrying mirror and wished it could tell her why the fuck it even existed. "What are you for?" she asked the little thing. "If not my dinner, someone else's? Maybe that thing outside wants to eat you—or maybe you'll kill it if it does."

She shut down an internal debate to toss the dish. Being a stranger in a strange land meant there were hundreds of customs she was oblivious to; perhaps the garlic was used to stave off vampires, or maybe its presence cleansed the air of old energy in the way her roommate abused white sage.

Jenny stepped away to mind her own business.

The suite had no television to keep her company, and a nonexistent phone signal chained her to an endless circuit of tapping the Wi-Fi icon. Hapless prodding and scrolling resulted in her giving up on the device altogether. She tucked it under a flat, perpetually moist pillow, and leaned against the headboard with hard eyes examining its decorative posts. The same houndish faces sewn into the chairs were carved in each wooden post of her bed. They stared at her like dutiful guardians.

Their unmoving pupils kept watch throughout the night. Each time Jenny came close to falling asleep, she jolted back awake with a spike of paranoia; she felt that something else resided in the room with her.

She rolled her eyes. *At least the ghosts are dogs. That's kind of cute.*

To calm herself, she retrieved her phone and found the same newsfeed mummified from when she first landed in Ljubljana. She stored it away in frustration and plucked her father's pocket journal from her bag. She flipped to a random page with a huff. Neat scribbles of Slovenian phrases and their English translations fit perfectly between each line. "Keh-neh... Kuh-jee..." She squinted, the honey-colored glow of her overhead sconce useless as lighting, and none of the switches turned the damned thing off. "*Knjižnica?* Sure, dad. I'd love to go to a library here. Can't even read the signs, let alone a fucking novel."

Jenny dropped the book off the side of her bed and drew the damp covers over her chin. Minutes dripped by. Her eyes became so used to the darkness; she could draw the desolate room from memory. The absolute quiet kept her mind stimulated. Wispy exhales from her nostrils further irritated her with every breath. "Even if I get six hours—" Jenny said to herself while trying to ignore the infinitesimal movements under her eyelids. "I can just nap at his house." An hour later, the goalpost shifted. "Even if I get five hours. Even four's not so bad."

She finally found something other than silence to focus on. A dense copse of trees outside rustled with intention, as though engaged in the midnight ritual of a flouncing dance. Their arms spread wide, and their canopies shook in time with the beat of swarming gusts. The ambiance helped lull her into a complacent meditation the more she focused on it.

Her consciousness steadily dropped into the back of her skull, and, after a while, her busy brain stopped reminding her that her toenails were slowly growing at the rate of fossilized molasses—or at the pace of a limbless torso dragging itself by its teeth.

In the quarter-second between wakefulness and succumbing to the abyss, a distorted bark erupted an inch from her face.

Her eyes shot open. The sound set her heart aflame. Paralyzed, she drank in the interior of her bedroom; each muddy shadow, each swath of darkness reminded her of something equally terrible. The shape of her curtains twisted into lanky, big-headed aliens, and the posts at the end of her bed turned into snarling beasts. The very idea of receiving a nourishing rest dissipated the longer she stared on.

Jenny's heartbeat subdued into a calm state and reminded herself of Exploding Head Syndrome—an ailment that affected her father much worse than her. A strange sound, be it a siren or a voice, resulted from some hypnagogic side-effect of drifting to sleep.

The subtle sound of scraping toenails tickled the hallway. Knowing she was fully awake, her eyes watered.

She trained her ear to the sound and searched for any sign that it came from another guest and found nothing. Rhythmic panting dropped from the lungs of a slow-moving beast, its gait heavy and tired.

Its presence disappeared after wandering farther down the hall. Pardon the occasional tap of leaf-against-stucco, a dead silence returned heavy as ever.

Her father once told her of a ghost story that followed him since he was a kid. Jenny remembered the image of her dad, bedridden and immobile from the waist down, scratching the top of her head as she sat against his gatch bed. "Slovenia is *too* beautiful," he said with a twinkle in his eye and a limpness to his touch. "So spirits, they never want to leave. There's no reason to. My childhood home, the one your grandmother's brother built, was full of the dead. No, it's okay. They weren't mean or scary. I remember one lady, she was blue, and she smiled at me every time I saw her. She'd disappear right after, but everyone believed me. They said they saw her, too. It's like having another mom, one that was always nearby. One day, I'll go back to that house—even if that means being a ghost to get there again."

Jenny leaned forward, rubbed her eyes, and sighed at the dogfaces staring from either post. "No offense," she stood up to fetch twin pairs of panties from her bag. "But I have *got* to get some sleep and you guys are creepy as hell."

She draped the carved beasts, forsook the thought of ghost stories, and relished the soft touch of slumber as it massaged her unconscious.

3

"Something is happening." Jenny's mother said
calmly and without moving her lips. "Embody awareness."

*

There was enough sense in Jenny Novak's tired skull
for her to feel urgency when lying in the bed of a visibly
foggy bed-and-breakfast somewhere deep within a country
that didn't share her tongue.

Fog filtered between the cracks of swollen wooden
planks and smothered her during the night. She lifted her
head, took in a deep breath, and lamented at how sticky and
thick the air had become. Grasping her chest and moving her
body into an upright position, Jenny took a few moments to
recalibrate to reality. Her eyes stung and, no matter how
many times she blinked or rubbed, a calvary of tears never
arrived.

After a sharp exhale, she threw her legs over the bed
and hobbled like a newborn colt to the door.

A fleeting bolt of embarrassment ran through her
core. She wore the same outfit as yesterday and hoped
neither Sabiha nor Romeo would be awake at such an
ungodly hour to run into her. Jenny cast the guilt aside and
popped the door open. She peeked her head out and found
the entire hallway had been flooded with the same fog
perforating her room.

She eased one naked foot into the hallway before assuring the other. Anemic glows from the sconces barely lit her path. To her left was the window at the hallway's end, but something seemed off.

Jenny hurried to the portal, but no longer felt a chill. Iron nails stapled the corners of each curtain to the wall; it looked like someone sewed the fucking things together.

"What the hell?" The material was so taut, it was like clawing the wall itself. After a minute of hapless grasping, she cursed and abandoned the project.

The cadence of shuffling froze her. She turned to see a figure swiftly traipsing through the fog. Its shape cut through and left a temporary trail of voided space behind it.

Jenny stopped herself from calling out. Fear hadn't won yet, but an aberrant curiosity clambered to the forefront of her anxious mind.

The figure disappeared for a moment before reappearing with a groan of confusion. It scratched its balding head and ambled towards her, squinting and mumbling. Jenny flattened herself against the corner and swallowed hard.

It asked a question in Slovenian, and it felt as though someone pricked a needle into Jenny's inflated heart.

"Hello. Um," she shook her head and pulled away from the curtained window. "I don't understand. Sorry. Ah, erm, *se opravičujem...*?"

An older gentleman reduced the distance between them. He babbled in his native language, received a blank stare, and pointed through the fog.

"Does this normally happen? Is it... Coming from downstairs?"

He sighed, exasperated, and reached out to grab her wrist. She pulled away. "Hello! *Hello-o-o*?" The tone reminded her of the American sitcoms she grew up with—the same shows the world presumably also grew up with. He jabbed the air and waved her over.

"Okay, just don't touch me. What is it?" Jenny moved when he did but kept a cautious pace to monitor his actions. The man moved with a wide, struggling gait. His right hip locked each time he put pressure on the corresponding foot. A breathy grunt dropped with every other step, leaving a wake of hot breath. Over time, she developed the assurance that, should he ever turn around and try to grapple her, she could easily out-maneuver him—probably just by moving three inches to the right.

By the time they reached the staircase, they bonded over the fact that there wasn't one. Jenny scoffed. "Okay. What the fuck?"

He threw his hands up in frustration. "*What the fuck, yes?*" he repeated in a thick Eastern European accent. They were finally on the same page. Then, in his native tongue, a long string of potential explanations that didn't help her at all.

Jenny muttered, "Yeah, yeah. Okay." She bent a knee and grazed the seamless wooden planks that met with one another. Dust caked the tips as if they've been set forever. "This isn't right. Shit. I'm dreaming." She shook her head, adopted a placid smile, and stood upright. "It's okay, friend! You're dreaming!"

"What?"

"Dreaming!" She mimed a pillow with both hands and exhaled. "*Honk-shoo, honk-shoo.*"

A subtle grin curled the man's lips, and he huffed a raspy laugh. "No..." Before he could be convinced otherwise, he placed both hands on his waist and made a contemplative expression. "Okay." A thumb dove toward his solar plexus. "Vasilij."

"Ah. I'm Jenny."

"*Jenny,*" he bounced a nod. "Jenny? What the fuck, what the fuck?"

She lifted her shoulders and turned back to face the rest of the hallway. "Dunno, mate. Let's try to see if someone else is home."

Jenny placed her ear against room two, heard nothing, and knocked anyway. Vasilij stood guard behind her and tried to blink away the stinging fog. After a second attempt, she tried for the handle. It spun in her palm and allowed entrance without a fight. She looked to her new acquaintance and called him over, but he groaned out of rightful hesitation and strafed farther away as if to say, *yeah, I'll just stay right here, thanks.*

"Suit yourself."

Through the fog, room two appeared to be identical to hers. After her eyes accommodated to the silver veneer, she realized room two was *exactly* hers—her black panties draping the bed posts solidified the revelation. "Wait." She checked behind her shoulder to find the door sealed tight and paused to consider the circumstances. The ground welcomed *her* bag and *her* father's notebook. Her phone remained upright where it had been hours before. She checked the bathroom and saw her fluoride-free toothpaste. The bristles of her green travel toothbrush were still damp.

She pocketed the phrase book. "Okay, I—I'm room nine. I go to sleep, I wake up, I walk outside, look at the..."

She slowed her manic pacing, turned her eyes to the covered window adjacent to the door, and marched. A pair of heavy terracotta-colored curtains matched the set of the hallway window. "No staples or nails in this one," Jenny said to herself. "So, what's going on? Why that one and not this one?"

Both hands gripped the material. The curtains rattled on their rusted rings, and her throat dropped into her bladder. On the other side of the window lay another identical set of curtains, separated by a shared panel of glass. She touched the dusty surface and withdrew her hand before jogging to the door. After haphazardly swinging it open, she called for Vasilij.

The hallway was empty, pardon the ever-present and spectral fog. "Nice one, dude. Where'd you go?"

"Hello?!" a new, female voice shouted from within the dense mist. The sound of clopping high heels acted as radar pings. Jenny reduced into the room but didn't shut the door. The woman asked, "Did I hear someone, or am I going insane?"

"Hey, I'm over by room..." Jenny blinked, the number completely lost on her. "Two, or nine, I guess? I'm not sure."

"No matter," the woman said as she emerged from the veil. "I see you. I see you." She was a tall, gaunt woman with dainty square glasses perched just above the tip of her nose. She pushed up her spectacles and lifted her chin. In an accent Jenny struggled to identify as either Swiss, German, or a combination of either, she said, "Oh! You're pretty!"

"Thanks. Have you, erm, noticed anything strange going on?"

"Obviously! This whole trip is a nightmare." The thin woman shook her head and scratched at her red bob. "I tell you. I've been up since four-thirty with this god-awful feeling in my stomach. I thought I'd get downstairs early, maybe eat some breakfast. Come to find out—"

"There's no staircase?"

She incredulously chuckled. "Precisely! I've lost my mind, haven't I? Or, perhaps, I suffered a heart attack in the middle of the night, and now I'm just dead. That's the easiest explanation, isn't it?"

Jenny disapproved of the inchoate theory with a tongue click. "If you had a heart attack, Vasilij and I had one, too."

"Vasil-*who*?" She assessed her environment. "Is that another guest? Friendly, I presume?" Jenny nodded.

The woman licked her lips in contemplation. "Well, we should keep a lookout for him. My name is Anna." She withdrew her glasses to wipe condensation away from its lenses.

"Jenny. Something else is strange."

"Only one other thing?"

Jenny cracked a smile. "Oh, I'm sure we'll find a *smörgåsbord* of strange things, but, yeah, you have to come with me."

"Naturally! Lead the way." Anna perked up and graciously examined the hallway interior, ready to charge down any other shadows with her painted claws or sharp, cloven hooves.

Jenny held the door open for her. "In here." The door creaked shut behind the two.

Anna tried to wave away the fog. "This is quickly becoming annoying."

"Check this out." She gestured to the window. "Look what's behind the curtain."

Anna's delicate fingers touched the glass. "Another room? Wait, there's another room behind..." She tried to angle for a better view, but there hadn't been as much as a crack between the second set of curtains. "Sorry. I'm just trying to make sense of it all. There should be the parking lot, or at least the woods next to it. Which room would this one be, then?" She tapped the glass twice with a square-tipped acrylic nail.

A wistful sigh. Jenny crossed her arms and kept her shoulders hiked in perplexed confusion. "I guess it'd be room ten or eleven, yeah?"

"No, it'd be room three." Anna blinked, then cocked her thin eyebrows. "This is room two, dear."

Jenny wandered to the low table she previously tossed her key on. The number 9 had been carved on its thick loop. She highlighted the matching bed posts with a swaying finger. "This is definitely my room. Note the, erm, *silk accouterments*." Both were draped with black panties to hide the hideous faces of the wooden hounds. "They don't have my name written on the tag, but I'll show you a matching pair I have on if you don't believe me."

"No need, dear. Well, that is curious, isn't it?" Anna lifted the key and inspected it in the orange light of the mounted sconce, half-expecting the number to shift once given the proper amount of attention. "There wasn't a young couple in here when you walked in?"

"Nope. Nobody." Jenny, stumped and suffering a growing headache, rubbed her stinging eyes. She chose not to exacerbate their trippy conundrum by mentioning the possibility of ghosts.

"Mm, no matter. We can settle this in a pinch. Come." She motioned for Jenny to join her. "It'll be just for a second. Come on! I'll go mental if we don't figure this out. I love mysteries, you know. Escape rooms, all of it. My sister's an author. She's going to be *so* jealous once I tell her about this—if she doesn't commit me to a mental hospital by the end."

Jenny couldn't deny her aching curiosity and indulged in her acquaintance's request. The two stepped out of the room, back into the whitened hallway, and hung in front of the plaque long enough for the door to seal shut.

Anna pursed her lips. "Oh." She looked at the opposite end of the hallway. "Wait, but I was near the... No, I was..." She danced in place for a handful of seconds before forcing an exhale.

"See, this is room nine now, but when I went in searching for other guests, it *was* room two. Right? When I entered the door that said room two, it just turned out to be *my* room. Underwear and all."

Even hidden behind the mist, Jenny could see how pale Anna became. Her already sallow features deepened, and every blink lasted a minute. "Huh. I see. I won't pretend any of that makes sense, but... Well, th-the door's shut now. Maybe we can just forget about it and move on? Find other people, if that's alright with you? I don't think I want to be alone."

Jenny crossed her arms and nodded. "Sure. Strength in numbers."

The woman turned to where she believed the staircase to be. The resolve in her voice slipped away the longer she spoke. "Should we try the stairs again?"

"No point, Anna," Jenny shook her head, a grim smile bereft of humor. "I can already tell you they won't be there."

A moment to collect herself. "What do you suggest, then? Should I just go back to my room? Will it even *be* my room? Should I just wait it out, try to sleep?" Then, in a mutter, "Or maybe even wake up."

The gleam in Jenny's auburn eyes sharpened. "Here, step inside." She stepped away from the threshold of room nine and pointed at the door. "Go inside, tell me if it's room nine, two, or... What room are you?"

"Five."

"Or room five. Go on. I'll be out here waiting."

She muttered a familiar German curse word and reached for the knob. "If I don't come back—"

"That's not going to happen. We're still in real life, you know. Those types of things don't happen in real life." Jenny assured her by offering a firm, almost comforting smile. "I'll be right here."

"A guinea pig," Anna exhaled. "That's all I am." A half-minute later, she disappeared into the room...

...and reappeared within the next breath, several paces behind Jenny and somewhere within the dense fog. Her jaw and both shoulders slacked. "*Demonic!*"

"Anna?"

"How is this possible?" Her heels stamped their way back to her. She carried with her an aura of extreme anxiety.

"I'm never going on vacation again, and if I am, it'll be Hawaii and not shitting Slovenia!"

Jenny hissed a laugh. "Of all places."

"It's cheap," Anna defended herself. "And beautiful."

"And don't forget haunted."

"This"—she widely gestured around her—"constitutes a little more than *haunted*. Cursed, maybe. Black magic, I'd suspect, due to its history."

Having nothing else to add, as Anna's theories were as valid as hers, Jenny cocked her eyebrows and forced herself to sober up. She took stock of the situation. The same parts of her brain that were exercised during coding sprints lit up as she plotted a mental map.

Anna spun on her heels to make sense of the labyrinth she had been lured in. "Maybe I should go back to church."

It didn't take long for Jenny to surmise a hypothesis. "You said room two was occupied by a couple. Yeah?" She stared down Anna to excavate an answer. "I doubt they left after I went to bed. Don't know anyone in their right mind who would go out there when it's still pitch black."

"Ah. You're saying they might still be around here. Okay, okay. I'm following you. Say, about those innkeepers..." Anna looked up at the a-frame ceiling. The fog had risen to the convex and hid the complex geometry of wooden rafters within. "Do you think they're below us? I mean physically, as in *literally* below us?"

"Yeah, I don't know. That's a good question," Jenny admitted and walked to the center of the hallway. She tapped the floor with the heel of her shoe. Two light *thumps*. "Anna, do me a favor and cover your ears."

"What?"

Jenny swallowed a quick influx of air, straightened her back, and shrieked—as loud as any victim in any horror movie, as loud as a tornado siren warning others to find safety. Her right foot stomped the ground and kicked up dust sprites as it pounded the wood. Anna gasped and knocked her glasses away while trying to shield her ears from the deafening sound.

"Good God!" Anna whined once the scream resolved. She watched as Jenny rubbed her throat; a hard grimace contorted her face. "Were you a banshee in a past life?!"

Each word came hoarse. "Can't be something that doesn't exist."

Massaging either temple, Anna mumbled, "So you don't believe in ghosts after all? That explains why you're having so much fun with all of this."

"I never said that. Also, does it really look like I'm having *fun?*"

"I mean..." She mimed the girl's desperate act.

Jenny rolled her eyes. "Listen."

They both transitioned to the quiet hope that somebody beneath them would respond to their pleas. Jenny imagined Sabiha banging the ceiling with the dull end of a broom, totally desensitized to the fog, screaming at her to quiet down. *We removed the stairs at night because they're too loud!* the old caretaker might yell in so many words. *They're too squeaky—it'll wake everyone up!*

The rubbery creak of a distant door pulled their focus. A gruff male voice shouted into the mist; his words angrily spouted in Slovene.

Jenny reached out as though the man could peer through the mist and accept her hail. "Hello!" The door slammed shut without another response. "Wait! Ah, shit." Her palm massaged the well of her throat. When she swallowed, a stinging sensation pinched the scorched muscles. "Probably for the best. He sounded like a dick, anyway."

"I'm not claiming to be a master of the language," Anna began. "But I do have a command over the most popular Slovenian curse words." She pursed her lips when Jenny shot a look her way. "What? There's a perfectly good reason to do so. As a tourist, it's nice to know when someone is calling you a bitch, or if they're asking you to suck their... You know?"

"Right, well, you're doing better than me. I've got *sorry* and *good night*. Oh! You wanna learn the word for 'library'?" Jenny asked Anna. She patted the pocket where her father's phrase book temporarily lived. "I've got a bunch of gems in here. For example..." She read from the book and butchered a long string of slurred syllables.

Anna frowned. "Sounded like gibberish to me. What does that one mean?"

"I asked you if you'd like to go to dinner with me. Oh, uh, not actually, though. I'm not—like, it's just a..."

"Settle down, sweetheart. You're too young for me, anyway. Do you happen to have another brilliant plan? We skipped from plan-B-to-Z, and nothing came from it."

Jenny's face winced from embarrassment. Coding often forced her to put Occam's razor into practice. "Sorry. I thought Romeo would bust through the floor with a fire ax."

"In this fantasy of yours, was he wearing shining armor?"

"Him and his trusty steed. I'm sure there's something we can do. There has to be."

The two turned to the expanse of hardwood where the staircase should've been. A creak, then a *thump*. Anna held onto her breath as though it were the only thing standing between her and being rescued from the sea of viscous fog.

A pair of voices prattled on from under the floorboard, their tonality lost against the barrier. A muffled argument raged on, its volume rising and falling without resolution.

"Is that them?" Anna asked.

"Maybe. I'm not sure."

Anna gestured for her to *do something, anything*.

It became clear to Jenny that Anna expected her to lead them to safety. If only she had a uniform and badge, she'd feel more obligated to respond to the call.

She dropped to her knees and placed her right cheek against the cold, dusty wood.

4

Closing her eyes helped her identify the voices.

Anna decisively hung back and watched Jenny with urgency building in her gut. With a raspy intone, she asked, "The owners, maybe?"

"Yeah. It's gotta be." Jenny replied. She coated her raw throat with a layer of saliva and prepared to once again shout for help. Her voice cracked as she yelled out, "Romeo?"

The argument paused to allow space for a man's voice to reply. It responded in muffled Slovenian.

"It's Jenny! Remember? I'm visiting my grandfather! I'm the, uh, Australian?"

The man exhaled his reply. "You are safe! That's—that's good!" It was as though he'd found a ladder and spoke with his mouth inches from the wood. "Who is also there?" Anna stepped forward with both hands clutching her chest and replied with her name. "The German? Okay, okay. Listen here to me."

Jenny interjected by clutching the wood flooring. "Romeo, what the hell is going on?"

"Please be nice. This is something that happens, erm, occasionally. But, still, it is very rare." His wife shouted at him in Slovenian and his tone tilted to exasperation. "The best thing for you to do is to wait. Go back to your room and sleep."

"Okay, wait. Romeo?" Jenny hesitated before continuing. Her heart trembled with so much force, her voice audibly shook. Cautious of her tone, she asked, grounded and cool, "What about the stairs?"

"They will return soon!"

"Soon...? Sorry, but how is any of this possible? Why is this happening to us?"

"Why does the sun set? It just does."

"That's... What? No, that's not a good enough answer. The fuck does that even mean?" She pulled away from the floor and patted dust away from her hands.

Anna cocked her shoulders and stood by as her new acquaintance settled into a low panic. Unable to think of a single comforting word, she covered her mouth with a curved finger and sank into her thoughts.

Steeling herself after a much-needed moment, Jenny lowered her face back to the ground and shouted to the caretaker, "So what, I'm supposed to just wait this out? It's—it's getting kind of hard to breathe in here, Romeo. It's getting hard to see."

An empathetic groan. "For us, as well. Our doors—they do not work. On the other side, another door. But, as I said, this happens occasionally. We are still getting used to it, but never quite will we ever truly become comfortable."

Jenny peeled away from the floor and turned to Anna. "Fucking hell. Well, what do you say? Sleep it off? Sounds like a super fun way to spend our vacation. Fuck," she ran a hand through her hair. "I need to call my grandfather."

Anna struggled to form a thoughtful reply. She wanted to ask if family was the reason Jenny was in this mess, and, if so, offer a bleak apology before squeezing out a few words of encouragement—something like *this'll all be over soon!*

Their gaze connected and a small twitch in Jenny's expression stopped Anna from speaking. It was an almost imperceptible shift from confusion-to-fear. With breath drenching her words, Anna asked, "What is it?"

A fleeting shadow materialized from the mist behind her, dark and formless at first, then all too human. Jenny squinted. "I think—"

A bulky object swung and missed; the gust displaced Anna's fox-red bob. She yelped and ducked to the ground, scrambled forward, and glued herself to Jenny like a startled dog.

The stranger remained silent, their stature tight, their lean form just as tall as Jenny. Their energy exhumed desperation, but their hesitation to try again read as calculating. Their shallow voice cursed, then babbled. Their short arms cocked the ceramic vase back to prepare for another strike.

"What are you doing?" Anna shouted. "Get away from us! Jenny—*do something!*" She wrapped her arms around Jenny's waist like a sloth hugging a tree.

"Get off of me! Come on, quick."

Jenny scampered in a bell curve back into the mist, narrowly avoiding another strike.

Their feet dragged along the wooden planks, and Anna's heel snatched against the edge of one bloated with age. Having reduced far enough away to gather a literal fog of war between them, she bit down on her lip to prevent an audible whine.

The assailant's soft tennis shoes flapped against the floor, each movement delicate and intentional. His voice finally registered as male as he called into the mist with gusto. An excess of adrenaline blemished his voice with vibrato; his tone reminded Jenny of a playground bully.

"He can't see us," Jenny's voice trickled into such a soft hush Anna could hardly decipher the words. The shadowy man etched his way toward them, blind yet determined, until the sound of one misplaced step alerted him of their approximate location. "Your shoes. Anna, take off your shoes."

"I—I..."

Jenny firmly clutched Anna's shoulders. In the quietest voice she could exhale, "Hey, hey, hey. Anna? Embody awareness. Okay? Pay attention to your surroundings and you'll be safe. Relax, alright?"

Anna gritted her teeth and leaned back into Jenny's torso for support. The woman deftly kicked one foot into the air and her shoe swam through the thick mist like a bird mid-dive. It clattered against the far wall. Both women shrank low when the assailant paused in his tracks. Anna dropped to her bottom and silently extracted the second shoe before tossing it in a similar direction with more confidence.

This act completely stole the stranger's attention.

They made out his hooded form lurking in the opposite direction, the bulky vase still firm in his grip.

Jenny helped Anna find balance and lifted her from the floor. Her hand lingered over the handle of room five and mentally commanded each finger to contract around it. The chilled metal, somewhat damp from the fog's humidity, only budged a half inch before stopping; the dull click helped reorient their attacker. "Shit."

A beastly roar reverberated from the man's throat. His voice knelled with dementation, like a child playing the part of an imagined demon *a little too well*.

"*Fuck!*" Jenny huffed and Anna concurred with a rising whine.

The stranger stomped in their direction, this time refusing to let the fog be an obstacle. In his disoriented blindness, he tossed his improvised weapon toward the sound of their hushed voices.

Ceramic split against Jenny's shoulder and dry soil exploded in a thick cloud around her. A yelp preceded a nasty curse. She lunged forward, deeper into the mist, with her eyes fixed to where room ten should be.

Anna shouted for her to stay close, to not abandon her, but the swarm of adrenaline saturating Jenny's spirit deafened the woman's plea.

The need for self-preservation swallowed her whole.

5

Room ten, as Jenny expected, was just room nine in disguise.

The door had no peephole installed, so she lost the opportunity to check on Anna. A desperate scuffle immediately filled her with intense regret.

"No!" the red-haired woman shouted. "Get away from me! Bastard!"

Jenny prioritized finding a weapon of her own—maybe a dried-out fountain pen from the desk drawer. *No*, Jenny swallowed hard and pressed her forefingers against her third eye. *I need damage.*

The bruise on her right shoulder swelled in a beautiful yet sickly purple miasma. It was the tattoo of a galaxy she belonged to, one of spiraling arms that broke off into brown clouds, each tinted with yellow, and marred by a thin gash of scarlet. She refolded the short sleeve of her pleated cream crop, once acceptably filthy by just having slept in it, and patted away a chunky collection of dirt that clung to the material.

"I can sleep it off. The door's locked, so I can just..." Jenny mumbled. She lamented over how dry her throat had become and rushed to her backpack. After draining a plastic water bottle, her eyes fell onto the stack of euros that suddenly registered as the garnish to a very funny joke. "Like I'm going to give Sabiha my fucking money after this."

Jenny lowered herself onto the edge of the mattress and habitually crinkled the body of the plastic bottle. Sharp crackling, slow in its release, interrupted the near silence of room nine. She hadn't heard Anna scream or cry since. *Maybe she followed my example. Found the nearest room and kept low.*

"Jesus," she said out loud.

Her sights turned to the still-opened curtain of her window as her adrenaline calmed to a familiar state. Butterflies aggressively bumped into the walls of her gut, with a few escaping up her esophagus or fleeing to her heart. Either leg moved autonomously, pulling her closer to the window, and stopped just as the tip of her nose pressed against the cool glass. Two rows of steam shot downward like ghostly stalactites.

Amongst the ambiance of creaking pipes, a low vocal murmur droned from beyond the window. Its cadence rattled with natural pauses, with organic convexes and lilts. Jenny lifted a pawed fist to the window and rapped against the glass with cautious regard; she was kind enough to be quiet, not wanting to interrupt someone else's conversation, but careful enough to pass off the sound as background ambiance.

The idea of courtesy, cute and appropriate in any other scenario, soon drained from her spirit. She needed help. *Anna* needed help. The knocking mutated into solid strikes.

Using the meat of a balled fist, the glass jittered with each pound. The murmuring ceased, but Jenny did not. She refused to pull away until whoever was on the other side opened their curtains to reveal themselves to her.

Each ring caught against the rusting rod, but a wrinkled hand eventually shoved one of the flowing orange curtains aside.

A balding, elderly man searched Jenny's face for familiarity. A sharp knot rose from the crown of his skull and the sight drew her eyes on more than one occasion. She mouthed a greeting, and he placed a soft hand against the window. His spongy voice barely penetrated the glass. "*Ah-h-h.* You too?"

"Yeah," Jenny reached out in solidarity and placed both palms forward. "Have you tried leaving?"

"What?"

A little louder: "Have you... *Have you tried leaving your room?*"

"They're all my room," the man's voice swelled. "Aren't they?"

Jenny humored his statement, but she shook her head in the negative. "This one is *definitely* mine."

"D-do you want to meet outside?" The intonation of his voice dipped out of clarity, but Jenny pieced his question together.

"That's—*no*, that's not a good idea."

Surprised, the man's bony shoulders slumped. "No?"

"A man is outside." Jenny read his expression and repeated herself with more effort. "He... *Look.*" She angled herself to the old man and revealed her fresh wound. The skin raised in a grotesque bump and blood speckled the sleeve.

He swallowed so hard a slither of saliva visibly traveled below his pronounced Adam's apple. "Oh, dear." The man scratched the back of his neck and searched the sill for a mechanism to open the window. "O-okay, well," he spun on his heels and started toward the identical waist-high desk allotted to his room.

Jenny backed away from the shared window as soon as he lifted the tiny chair above his head. "Christ," she whispered before parroting the same curse as a shout when the man tossed it through. A deafening crash, a waterfall of glass. Both palms cupped her mouth, and she slouched with disbelief shrinking her. "Holy shit. Okay, that... Wait, hold on."

The old man lingered in the opened portal. "Why?" She could finally make out the fine grain of his soft voice.

"The glass, dude. Don't hop over, yet."

"It's not going to be me hopping over anything, *dude*." He spread his wiry arms outward and tossed a shrug from his crooked back. A pink dress shirt draped over his torso like a tarp, especially ill-fitting around the wrists and neck. "That was all my strength for the month. It'll take me weeks to recover!"

Jenny conceded. "Yeah, alright." She searched the floor for shards large enough to claim as a weapon, found none, and resolved to break a leg off the thrown chair. Returning to the window, she brushed away shards of glass and tentatively vaulted over the sill.

Swiping away errant debris from her denim jeans, she immediately jumped at the chance to share theories. "Okay, so, you've already seen how weird all this is, yeah?" He shrugged while she inspected his room. Two large duffels, their brand familiar. A hard case with a large, rounded bottom was meant for an acoustic guitar. A small collection of snack wrappers and an unopened bottle of white wine laid on the floor next to the nightstand. "Who were you talking to?"

The man searched the large pockets of his light-tan slacks to retrieve a newer model phone. It looked foreign against his wrinkled flesh. "Not a soul. Damned thing has a hard enough time finding bars in the states, let alone out here in the sticks. I'm just recording some voice clips, that's all. What room are you?"

"Nine. You?"

"Ten, myself. I guess I'd be... Across the hall from you? Oh, I don't even want to waste my energy on figuring out how this whole thing works." He lowered his head. "But, no, I'm just here by myself. Leaving, erm, voice memos. Snippets of songs—lyrics and such. Are you able to contact anyone? Police, or...?"

Jenny furrowed her brow and tensed her posture. "You tell me. Your phone's nicer than mine. Unless they have public wi-fi here, I'd reckon our cells are useless. I only saw a private network, but I can't crack the password." Her spine straightened as she grazed the room for a note. She bypassed her new acquaintance and flung open the drawer to his desk. "Damn."

"Can't find anything?" the man asked, seemingly already knowing the answer. "So, what are we to do 'til the fog rolls away? Meditate? Starve? What do the owners of this place have to say about all of this?" He crossed either arm over his bony chest and looked at the ceiling. "They better not ask me to pay."

"You said you're from America, huh?" Jenny severed the spiraling train of thought and approached his door to check the security of his lock latch. "Never been, never really wanted to go. Whereabouts?"

"I-I'd rather focus on what's going on here, if that's okay." He twisted his lips into a humorless smile and cocked his shoulder. "You know. Priorities."

"Sure. Well, you broke the window," she cocked an eyebrow. "And, just a few minutes ago, someone threw a potted plant at me. After that..." Her stomach blanched when she considered how she abandoned Anna. The man leaned in, expecting an explanation to her sudden, visible stress. Jenny scratched her temple and organized her thoughts out loud. "I've met two other people—two other *friendly* people. Ones who don't want to kill me."

The old man stuck his head into her room. "Mm, as far as you know. What happened to them?"

"One disappeared, and the other one... We separated after the attack. I hope she was clever enough to do what I did and Scooby-Doo her way out of danger."

He chuckled and turned to face Jenny. "It is a lot like Scooby-Doo, isn't it? We even have the *coup de grâce*—a real life *villain!*"

"I'd rather be in Yogi Bear. Something comforting."

"With food," the man raised his brow and sucked his lips.

Playing along, "Scooby-Doo has food, too."

"Not if Shaggy finds it first."

Stress melted away from him in waves, falling off his thin, broad shoulders and splashing to the wooden floor below. A smirk hung on the corner of her lips for a while, long after their banter ended.

Feeling secure enough with her around, he invited her to sit and relax.

"What's that? You'd like me to sit on *the chair*?" she asked with sarcasm curled around each syllable.

"Ah, well," he flustered while gesturing toward the mattress. "The bed's fine, I guess, as long as you don't mind."

"You're alright. D'you play?" She nodded to the guitar case. Confidence emanated from him like visible odor lines from one of the cartoons they bonded over.

He said, "Just about fifty years. I'd like to make it to fifty after all this."

"Holy shit. Fifty years? Oh, I didn't mean for that to sound, like, rude or anything."

"Rude? No, no. Not at all. Actually, 'holy shit' is right. Every time I tell someone my age, I get verklempt." He clutched the center of his chest. "What about you?"

"What about me?"

"Do you play? If not guitar, maybe something else?"

Jenny blinked. "If you're asking if I have any discernible skills, that's a no."

His voice softened in disbelief. "You must have something, dear. Everybody has something."

Her eyes searched the ground. For a moment, she forgot about all the troubles waiting for her outside. "I code, but I wouldn't say I'm a prodigy. I suppose I reckon myself a good leader. Y'know, delegating tasks and that."

"It's easy to subvert stress when you have other people to prioritize first."

Sinking further into the cot, she admitted, "Is that right? If that's the criteria, maybe I'm not so good at it, after all. Hey, I have an idea."

"I'm all ears."

"What if we tear the floor away? Plank-by-plank, 'til we see the white of Sabiha and Romeo's eyes?"

Without humoring her, he diverted and scratched the knot on his head. "I really just wonder how they're going to explain this."

"Believe it or not, I talked with them just before the attack. I swear! Through the floor, right where the stairwell should've been. They said—get this, mate: they said this whole thing 'happens occasionally'."

"Otherworldly fog was *not* listed in the ad." His sharp fingernails scratched at the low thread count sheets and he exhaled after a moment of frustration. His eyes pawed at the dog-like faces etched in either bed post. "Those are curious, aren't they?"

"Romeo said they used to board dogs here."
"Hm. Must be why the rooms are so small. Those bathrooms, not much to them. Looks like they installed a shoddy toilet and shower head and called it a day." He chuckled, then quieted down as if saddled by guilt.

Jenny asked, "You alright?"

"I'm tired, you know? Yes, because of whatever *this* is"—he vaguely gestured around him—"but also... Ah, never mind. It's not your cross to bear. Let's get back on track."

She agreed with a small smile lifting her lips. The man's depressed energy made her want to act as his therapist. If ever put in the situation, she could muster up a select few buzz words.

"Too much seems off. You said you were attacked by someone? If that's true, don't you think it's best to just stay put? I really don't see another option. Hiding doesn't have to be all that bad. Without that window, we've really opened the floor space. We've got the presidential suite now!"

Jenny's eyes searched the air for a response while a smile faded from her face. After a long pause, she carefully deliberated on each word as they appeared in her throat. "Earlier, you said something about prioritizing other people."

"Something like that."

"It's just—I don't want to see anybody die today."

The man sobered. His right hand twitched, as though stopping himself from reaching out to console his new acquaintance. She wondered if he had ever been a father. He sputtered a nervous laugh and asked, "Die? Who's going to die?"

"I've met two very nice people—sorry," she reached out to touch his forearm. He staved off the crimson sheen that dared coat his cheeks. "*Three* very nice people who deserve safety. You should stay here."

His fingers found their way back to the knot on his head. "I'd like to inform you it was never my intention to leave. So, you're going back out there? To do what, exactly?" The man nearly ran out of breath. "At least tell me you've come up with a plan?"

She stood up from the mattress and stretched her back, using the splintered chair leg as a brace against the bottom of her spine. Patting the blunt end against her palm, Jenny said, "Our rooms are connected, yeah? Without this window, there's less separation, which means more safety. If things get hairy, I just find the nearest door and *boom*. We're reunited in the presidential suite."

A disconcerted expression twisted his face while he combed through her theory. "Is that how it works? Others can come in with you, I'm assuming?"

"As long as I'm the one to open the door." She stated her theory with so much confidence, any doubt seeped from the old man's spirit.

"Well, if that's your master plan, I'll be here twiddling my thumbs. Oh, uh—ma'am?"

"Jenny," she coyly corrected him.

"Yes, Jenny. Do you have any food?"

Her gaze hardened with the revelation that, at some point, anyone caught on the second story will run out of food. "Sabiha gave me a metric fuck ton of halva if you want it."

He scrunched his face. "I hate tahini. The smell of it alone."

"I get it. I have a few granola bars in my bag."

"Oh, granola? And you have enough to share?"

She blinked twice and batted the length of wood against her palm. "As long as you can climb through." He pouted and lifted his scrawny arms as if to say *but, I'm just a poor old man*. "If you're desperate, there's always the garlic."

He dropped his arms and rolled his eyes. "Definitely not, missy. It's never a good idea to eat someone else's offering."

Jenny tilted her head. "Wait, what? That's an actual *offering?* Like, for a god, or something?"

"Seems to be trending that way. Our little friends," he nodded to the carved bed posts that stared at them with gaping mouths and hard eyes. "They might have something to do with this, too."

"On top of everything else," Jenny said with an eyeroll. "Ghost dogs and old gods."

"Well, I'm not on the up-and-up with *all* the Greco-Roman deities, but the idea certainly sounds familiar. There's quite a remnant of believers here, especially when one enters rural territory. Beliefs could've been carried here from Turkey, maybe as far as Iraq. These ancient gods tend to stay alive by latching onto whoever will answer the call, don't they? Cultures borrow them, repurpose them—but they never quite die." He nodded to the shallow dish of dried garlic. "Especially when someone keeps feeding them."

Jenny seethed and shook her head. After stretching, she said, "Yeah, it's all too spooky for me, mister...? I'm sorry. I probably should've asked for your name when you asked for mine."

"Just Martin. No honorifics necessary."

"Okay, then, Just Martin. You're a musician and a historian. Who knew?"

Martin's nostrils flared when he grinned. "I'm writing an album as we speak, and I'm traveling the world to do it." Jenny floated to the center of the room. He took her silence as permission to continue his ramble. "But, Slovenia." The man shook his head and sighed. "This place has been difficult."

"Hence the voice memos?"

"Hence the voice memos. Okay, Jenny," he lifted himself up from the bed with a grunt and walked her to the door. "I'll lock it behind you."

Jenny chewed on her bottom lip. "Should we have, like, a secret knock?"

"Now, that's a good idea. If you ever need respite, simply tap out a simple nine-eight polyrhythm at one-thirty-one beats-per-minute for two measures."

"Sure," a wild grin stretched her pill-shaped face. "Easy-peasy."

Martin did well to mask his smile. He held all the humor in his heart and converted it to joy as he said, "See you in a few minutes with all your new friends. I can't wait to meet 'em."

A single delicate motion from her forefinger and thumb slid the brass latch. Jenny cracked open the door, and, without a goodbye, disappeared into the thick, rolling mist like a raft pushed out to sea.

6

Any glee cultivated from meeting Martin sapped away as soon as the honey-coated fog touched her flesh.

A condensed column of light feathered through the hallway—a beacon struggling within a borderless sea of silver, broken only by the orange-glow of antiquated sconces. The tension of absolute silence bore its way into Jenny's bones, and the balmy humidity helped convince her she had somehow entered another dimension.

That light was alive.

It stroked away; its owner well-hidden. As far as she knew, there happened to be at least one other person in the hallway; they could've been a complete stranger, a real-life villain, or one of the other friendly faces she'd met along the way. Anxiety bulbed behind her sternum and a hundred words fought for supremacy, fighting to claim the rising impulse as their own. She wanted to shout for Vasilij, for Anna, but couldn't dare risk her own skin for the sake of potentially reuniting with an acquaintance she'd just met—especially if they'd end up useless against a psycho who found a thrill in hunting others down.

If throwing shit's all he can do, thought Jenny as she corrected her posture and suddenly appreciated the weight of the equipped chair leg. *Then, I might have an advantage. As long as I stay close to him... As long as he doesn't have any tricks up his sleeve.*

The beacon dissipated just as Jenny resolved her internal monologue. Though the idea that this bright light offered a semblance of heat was psychosomatic, she couldn't shrug away an oncoming shiver when it disappeared. Her hot breath churned the fog, and she ventured forward while sucking her lips to stifle her shaky breath.

One heel softly pressed into the floor before straightening out. The second mimicked the first, and the pair repeated the cycle until Jenny achieved what she considered a masterful grasp of stealth. She did as she told Anna, as Jenny's mother had imparted to her.

"You're smarter than everyone you've ever met," her mother once said. "At least, that's what you decided. Be a lone wolf—fine—but be smart about how you carry yourself. Embody awareness, and you'll always come out just fine."

Whether Jenny walked alone to the bus stop or met up with a new date, she did as her mother suggested. To the best of her ability, without having been taught by means of a visual guide or lesson plan, she embodied awareness—even if it meant walking away from a handsome man who gave her the ick or waiting an extra second before crossing the street.

Subtle movements twisted the mist. Their presence accosted her sympathetic nervous system; humanoid faces appeared and dissipated as soon as they formed; shadows swam by her as though she waded through a crowded train station.

Jenny tried to recall the concept of feeling calm. "You're fine," she repeated to herself. Her voice sounded flat once her words struck the air. "You're fine." By the time she drifted somewhere in the hallway's throat near rooms five and six, her own voice sounded foreign to her. "You're fine? Are you fine? Am I fine?"

A circus of fleeting shadows took up residence around her; sharp nails scratched the wooden floor and mangled with the shimmer of dog tags as spectral hounds bounced along the hallway.

Discerning whether these movements were born of paranoia or were actual physical entities crept its way to the top of her ladder of priorities.

When she blinked, the forms disappeared and only a sheet of white remained. The longer she stared into the mist, the more active her ghastly guests became.

These visions didn't pose an immediate threat, even if they lit her nerves on fire. She embodied awareness and relied on her gut to tell her whether she was in danger.

The only danger came from her continued distraction.

It became almost impossible for Jenny to compartmentalize reality from ghost stories, and if the hooded assailant still wandered the hallway, she feared she wouldn't be able to protect herself with a chair leg alone—especially if he used the cover of fog to camouflage himself.

Breathing too hard, moving incorrectly, or even allowing a single whined syllable to flee from her lips could cause another injury... Or worse.

The bruise on her right shoulder throbbed in time with her heartbeat, each pang a distraction that temporarily pulled her into fallacious territory. *I will not die,* she swallowed. *Especially not because of some cracked out whacko. I'm going to leave here and finally meet my grandfather and eat a bunch of good food and listen to stories about my dad when he was a kid and—*

"Oh, hello!"

Jenny took in a sharp breath of air, spun on her heels, and lifted the chair leg over her head: the shrunken image of Vasilij frightened her. Two strangers on either side lifted their hands over their faces as a flimsy veil of protection. "Jesus!" she cursed through a tight seethe while adrenaline blistered her core.

"*Se opravičujem!* Sorry, sorry!" Vasilij turned to his companions and attempted to calm them with dual thumbs-up. A nervous laugh dribbled from between his crooked teeth as he fought the mounted tension. He pointed at the two: a young couple wearing modern, stylish clothing. "Friends!"

"Friends?" Jenny cocked an eyebrow and waited for their reply.

The male, who wore a crisp teal hoodie and black skinny jeans, ventured a response. His accent fell somewhere within the United Kingdom. "Are we cavemen? Please tell me you speak English."

"Uh, yeah. I do. Do you?"

"Thank fuck." He lowered his voice and tilted his head forward. "I don't know what the hell this one's saying. *Ba-da-be-ba.* Christ, mate, he sounds like an engine won't start."

Jenny folded her brow. "Everyone here at least knows some English, *mate*. You've gotta be patient with them. How'd you end up with Vasilij?" Jenny moved a glance at the older man, who subtly perked at the mention of his name. His relieved smile, set on a square head and surrounded by a field of stubble, soothed her stressed heart like a cooling balm.

The second of the two jumped to answer—a young woman who kept immaculately coiled hair throughout the whole ordeal. "Oh, no shit, babe. You hear that? Vasilij is his *name*."

"Yeah," the young male rolled his eyes. "I get that now."

"I thought he was, like, trying to tell us something in Slovenian."

Jenny ignored the two with a hard eye roll. "Vas, are you okay?"

Vasilij blinked. He patted his torso before cocking a shrug. "Erm, yes. You okay?"

Jenny took the fated opportunity to draw everyone's attention to her. "Actually, no." She relinquished the grip of her weapon to her right hand and snapped twice with her left. This broke a conversation between Vasilij's new companions. "Hey, sorry. I'm sure all of that's interesting, but I feel compelled to let you guys know that there's a fucking psycho killer lunatic running around." She used her free hand to roll up her sleeve. The young woman made a sour face and looked away. "And he did this to me."

The male asked, "Did he throw a shoe at you?"

"A—what? A shoe?"

"We found a shoe over"—he twisted his torso and searched the foggy room—"thereabouts." His finger aimlessly pointed away from them.

"No, not a shoe. A pot, or something. My point is," she shook her head, leaned in, and dropped her voice. "He's dangerous and we need to stick together. Look, including you two, you're the—*fifth?*—people I've met here. Five-out-of-eleven rooms have been friendly. I-I think we should all stay together."

The posh girl said, "Four." Jenny paused with her mouth agape. After shaking her head, the new acquaintance expounded. "Christopher and I are in room two. So, that's only, like, four-out-of-eleven."

This correction knocked Jenny off-kilter for a few seconds. She stroked her lips with the fingers of her free hand. The tip of the broken chair leg rested on the wooden floor.

"I don't know what your plan is," the young woman continued. "Or, like, if a *plan* even needs to exist. Seriously! If what you're saying is true, the solution is quite simple, isn't it?"

Jenny's eyes hardened. "Go ahead."

"Just stay inside your room, lock it tight, and wait for it to be over."

Jenny's nostrils flared. "No, no. It's more complicated than that. It's... Why are you out here if you're telling me to stay inside?"

"Um, because we just woke up," the girl scoffed and looked up at her boyfriend. "And we have no idea what's going on, so we peeked our heads out here, threw on some clothes, and met up with..." She didn't bother to try pronouncing Vasilij's name again. "So, yeah. We're allowed to figure things out as we go, you know."

"Right," Jenny shook her head, blinked a few times, and returned her grip to the splintered weapon. "Do whatever you want, but if you two are going to go at it alone, there are a few things you should know."

This time, the boyfriend spoke. The confidence in his voice carried well throughout the hallway when everyone else chose to whisper. "Let me guess: the fog's evil? Yeah, sis.

I woke up and thought that shit. Legitimately, the first thought in my head was 'what the hell's up with this literal evil fog?'"

Admiration hugged the girlfriend as she commented, "Chris has watched, like, mostly every horror movie." She wrapped her arm around his and leaned her chubby face into his bicep.

Christopher nodded and pulled his partner closer to him. "Yeah, so, thanks for the heads up, but we're just gonna go back to our room."

Jenny bit down on the fat of her lower lip as soon as they walked away from her and Vasilij. "Room two," she said and watched the pair slow down. "Right?"

Christopher looked down at his expensive trainers, shook his head, and replied, "Yeah, yep. Why?"

Thoughts churned in her head as she visualized a hyper-dimensional puzzle slowly coming together. "Then you're connected to room one. No, not literally, but... Can you guys do me a favor? Just one favor, then you can go back to enjoying your vacation together."

The young girl pestered Christopher by tugging on the hem of his sleeve. She whispered something and he stifled a sigh. "Right, then. What is it?"

"Go to your room," a slow crease folded her forehead. "And break the window." The couple shared nervous laughter, and she added, "With a chair or something. *Anything*. Christ, I'll pay for the damage if anyone gives you shit about it." The girlfriend giggled and shrugged, excited about the prospect of risk-free vandalism in a foreign country. "I swear on my life, I'll pay for the window if it becomes an issue. You know, only after we escape from the *'literal evil fog'*."

Christopher shrugged his girlfriend away. "Don't humor her, Pennie. Penelope, babe—*no*. That's the actual stupidest thing I've ever heard," he said in a hush. "I'm not trying to get thrown into some Slovenian gulag for some silly shit we could avoid."

"Let me do it, then!" Jenny shook her head, the stress visibly mounting in the form of a hunched back and a desperate wince. "That guy can come back any second! Just being out here, he's probably listening to us right now!"

"Is that so?" Christopher puffed up his chest and shouted into the mist, "Come at me, bro. What's up, fucker? You'll hit a bird but not a grown man? Cowardice!"

The fog melted between the four like white dye bleeding into water. His outburst struck Jenny as childish, but she held her tongue knowing there seemed to be no effective way to get through to him. She looked at Vasilij, who shook his head with wide eyes and a furrowed bottom lip.

Pennie pulled away from her boyfriend, smacked him on the arm, and turned to Jenny with a non-verbal apology pasted on her face. "Sorry about Mister-Big-Man-Testosterone. Let me try to piece this together. You said my room is *connected* to room one? What'd you even mean by that? It's across from us."

"Something's happening here, and I don't know what. Something not normal."

Christopher called for her, and she crossed her arms with a sigh.

Pennie said, "Ignore him, sweetie. He believes in ghosts, but not curses and magic—thinks they only exist in fairy tales and movies. He's a total enigma, isn't he? Oh, and aliens! Chris definitely believes in aliens. But, yeah, you know, I love all that shit. Witchy shit, alien shit. The only reason we're here is 'cause of my favorite podcast."

Her boyfriend added, "She only knows about it 'cause of me and my mates."

She trekked on without acknowledging him. "People who've stayed here report missing time, ghost dogs, weird smells, the whole lot. Ugh! It's the best. So, whatever it is, lay it on me so I can eat it up."

Jenny examined the young woman's face while holding onto an unshakeable scowl.

Pennie's eyes were stained with eyeliner hastily wiped away the night before. Through either smudge, she could make out what would've been a pair of infallible double-flicks. Even while staying in a haunted bed-and-breakfast, even while being hunted down by a hooded madman, Pennie looked beautiful.

Jenny cleared her throat and spoke slowly. "My room—room nine—is connected to room ten by the window. You can crawl through, even though it should technically be—"

"—across the hallway?" Pennie pouted. "Okay, yeah. If that's true, that's mind-bending shit. I'm following you so far. " She cut off Jenny just as she opened her mouth to speak again.

Hesitation compressed Pennie's face. Her eyes traveled to the ceiling and searched through the mist for an answer to a question she could no longer internalize.

"What?" Jenny frowned.

"What if the killer's in room one, just chilling and waiting for someone else to show up? If we break the window and he's there, what do we do, then?"

Christopher nodded and clicked his tongue. "It's a trap, babe. This bitch is in on it, obviously." His pointer finger flung to Jenny and her eyes widened.

"No," Jenny scoffed and backed away with one step. "No, that's not true. I swear to God. How else would I have gotten this?" She gestured to her bruised shoulder. Vasilij clenched his fists. He visually tried his best to fish through the heated conversation for words he understood.

Pennie said, "That's a good point."

"Not a good point at all, babe," Christopher wrung his hands, his eyes glued to the armed woman. "Do we even know for a fact there's a killer? Have we seen him with our own eyes?" He didn't wait for his partner to answer. "Exactly. I've seen a movie once where some chick threw herself into a table just to convince the cops she was injured."

"I hate that one."

"That's a hot take, babe. Anyway, what I'm trying to say is—"

Jenny cut him off. "I'm not trying to kill either of you. This is lunacy." She lowered her head and blinked a handful of times before whipping her gaze back to Christopher. If the mist weren't muting the space between them, she could've sworn he flinched. "There's another woman. That shoe you found—it's Anna's. We threw it to distract him, to get away."

Christopher sniffed and crossed his arms. His square jaw lifted as he looked down at Jenny. "That's smart. A little too smart." He grinned when the accused tossed her head back in a groan. "Nah, I believe you, mate. You would've knocked my head in by now."

"Aw, babe," Pennie frowned and clung onto his arm. "That's so sad."

"Well, she is the only one with a weapon. No offense, Pens, but she could easily knock me out—*bow!*—then turn to you and with the sticky-pointy-end—*skrrsh!*—and, before Vazzy could even blink..."

Jenny turned to Vasilij. She almost snickered at the disbelief painting his face. He uttered *what the fuck?* under his breath and his acquaintance agreed with a shrug. "Look," she stepped forward and lowered her voice. "The longer we stay out here, the more we risk our skins. I think..." Her eyes fell to the broken chair leg, and she bit her lower lip. "I think we should find him before someone else gets hurt."

A palpable silence stiffened the empty space between the four. Pennie tilted her head. "You want to murder someone before *they* murder someone?"

"I mean, that's self-defense one-oh-one."

"What, are you a cop, or something? Nah, you don't have the look. Babe, massage my palm?" A thick, gold bangle slid down her scrawny wrist after sticking out her hand. Bright-orange acrylic nails completed the look of someone who didn't belong anywhere near the woods. "So, sweetie, that's not the best plan I've ever heard. Honestly, at the end of the day, Chris and I are here to explore nature and eat weird food. We're going to Croatia in a few days."

Her boyfriend interjected, "There's a sick castle up there, supposed to be haunted by some asexual monks." He wrapped either hand around hers and massaged Pennie's palm with his meaty thumbs. Her shoulders relaxed with every short stroke. "You know, the goal of visiting haunted houses is to remain a visitor, not become a resident."

"Babe!" she stomped. "That's so poetic!"

He smirked and shrugged one shoulder.

Two conflicting narratives battled against one another inside of Jenny's soul: one wished for her to be a hero, to track down the man who attacked her and Anna. The other understood both Martin and Pennie were correct about her leaping forward with an inflammatory, ill-thought-out plan. They both insisted she stay hidden and stay safe.

She grimaced when remembering how quickly she abandoned Anna.

The wooden chair leg became heavy, the material dissonant against her clammy skin. For a quick instant, Jenny saw herself from the outside looking in—a twenty-something with poor posture holding a piece of wood while hatching a grandiose plan of revenge. In another world, it was her own father who stood where she stood.

If he'd never been injured, the two could have visited Slovenia together, and, as soon as the fog started to roll in, he would've stepped up as a leader.

She exhaled the shame from her lungs. If her grandfather were here, he'd be rallying everyone to safety while fighting off the demons that lurk within the mist. In any scenario, she tended to be the weakest link—someone who needed to be saved just as much as any of the others they happened upon.

Jenny mentally shoved her master plan into a shredder. The chair leg suddenly reduced to a prop rather than a weapon. She tentatively asked the couple, "So, uh, you're here because of a podcast?"

Pennie looked to Christopher, almost for permission to speak. He shrugged his wide shoulders. "Yeah," she said. "It's so great. It's called *Folklore & Fuckery*. They had a whole episode about Slovenia and all the spooky shit that happens here."

"Was evil fog one of them?" Jenny glanced at Vasilij, who blinked as his response.

Pennie dug through her memory with a pouty lower lip. "Um, no. There's like, some bitch with one big foot that can transform into different animals. That's all I can remember, really. Oh, actually"—it looked as though both Pennie and Christopher simultaneously remembered a particular detail—"there's a segment about this place. That's how we knew to stay here."

Jenny frowned. "This place specifically?"

"Yup. I can't pronounce it in Slovenian, but it translates to something like 'middle of the road kennel'. Sweets, do you remember how it went?"

Christopher scratched his upper lip and said, "This place used to breed dogs and offer 'em up for slaughter. Sacrifices, wasn't it?"

Jenny's eyes darkened, and her shoulders slacked. "Jesus. So, this place really could be haunted, but by a bunch of dead dogs. That tracks. I feel like I... " She hesitated. "Maybe we're on some sick fucking Slovenian game show?"

Christopher snorted. "Like them ones in Japan? Yeah, that *would* be sick. You ready to bounce, Pens?" He squeezed her hand, and she shuddered, as if shaking off the chill that rolled up her arms. She nodded and he silently bid Jenny and her Slovene sidekick *adieu*.

Vasilij gravitated closer to Jenny and watched the young couple fight their way through the fog and return to their room. They used their phones' built-in flashlights to excavate their path.

"Just you and me, eh, Vas?" Jenny raised her brow. He squinted, lost for a reply. "Oh, hold up. Here... Give me one... Second." She tucked the table leg under her armpit and extracted the phrase book from her pocket. The pages fluttered until she landed on the closest phrase her father had scribed. It read, *Are you alone?* followed by the equivalent in Slovenian. "*Sam.* I hope I said that right. You, me. *Sam.* Alone. *Sam.* Alone."

"Alone," Vasilij repeated with some recognition. His head nodded and watched the English couple bob through the suffocating fog, strobing along the way like a condensed rave hidden within a spectral ocean.

A door slammed, and the streak of light redirected toward it. The couple's voices overlapped to create a disharmonious staccato, one that echoed through the long hallway in an incoherent babble. Jenny shouted, "Guys?!"

Vasilij stiffened. The tough skin of his palm gripped her wrist, and she coughed an airy yelp.

Jenny tried to pull away, but his already tight grip closed like an iron vice. She hissed, "What, Vas? *What?!*"

His pointer finger pressed against his mauve lips to shush her. She focused on the direction Vasilij pointed: farther down the hallway, back to where the staircase should've been, where rooms one and two were located.

She kept her attention on the dissipating light until the mist overtook the swaying beacon altogether. The bassy reverberation of wood-against-wood and the following soft click of a door set her on edge. Jenny reacquainted herself with the splintered weapon as though it was her best friend.

No more voices, no more footfall—even Vasilij's typically labored breaths relegated to slow, deliberate exhales.

A thought swam in the shallow pool of Jenny's consciousness, a near-psychic predilection that stunned her when it manifested into reality: the shrill squall of Pennie's voice.

Jenny tensed and started to lift herself from the floor, but Vasilij anchored her back into a low crouch. "Let go of me!" she hissed while he shook his head in rapid pivots. "Let—let go of…"

"N-no, please," he pleaded. "Here. You, me, here. No *sam*, no alone."

A final tug freed her from the man's grip. Every ounce of security drained from his face. Jenny wasn't sure whether he feared for his life or hers at that moment, but Vasilij's hopeless expression lagged her. She stood several feet from him, fully erect and looking down at the limp man like a dog groveling for food.

"No alone. No alone. Please, Jenny."

Breath flooded her lungs at the mention of her name. "Fine," she heard herself say. "Whatever. Okay, Vasilij. I'll stay with you."

He blinked a few times, bounced a nod, and dropped a heavy sigh from his dry mouth.

Vasilij licked his lips and pushed himself away from the ground, struggling to find footing while his heart arrhythmically tittered. Jenny extended a hand, and he gratefully accepted the gesture. As he looked up to thank her, the mist behind her darkened and the solid sound of impact pinched his heart. A damp spray of viscera traveled onto Vasilij's face, framing his broad forehead and pouty lips. The soft hand he accepted tensed, then fell flaccid. Her body mimicked soon after.

Jenny's form collapsed onto Vasilij, who attempted to hold her upright as if he were Atlas himself. Sustaining her weight while dealing with the unprecedented shock of the attack quickly wore away at his energy. He slowly folded backward into the cold, hardwood floor. Her unmoving corpse pressed onto him in a macabre union of affection, of farewell.

He remained still for as long as he believed necessary.

-32-

Vasilij had been a young man with a strong heart and a sharp mind in June of 1991. News of his country's independence filled him and his family with hope for the future, as well as a thin veil of trepidation regarding how Yugoslavia would take the news. Even while he, his brother, and his father shared celebratory drinks, a low-level current of anxiety kept their conversation grounded.

They talked about their neighbors in Croatia, how they simultaneously achieved independence. "We are like brothers and sisters, really," his father stated with his top lip draped over the edge of a shot glass. "A family. The Muslims, the Christians. Even by the old gods, we are like a family. Nobody—*NOBODY!*—deserves to be squashed under a single thumb!"

Vasilij watched as the shot glass dropped to the table edge-first. A scuff marked the old, fragile varnish.

A single, restless night later, the Slovene people were on high alert. They were hastily equipped with brutalist weapons borrowed from Israel and rushed to the border to stop an invading convoy of tanks departing from Belgrade. News of light injuries, crushed vehicles, and obliterated buildings reached the inland.

Vasilij and his brother, Samuel, were loaded into a repatriated school bus and whisked off to the Croatian border on the first of July, nineteen-ninety-one.

Sparse brick buildings and tall, skinny trees filled hills that subtly rolled through Slovenia and into Croatian territory. The further the bus drove, the denser the foliage became. A single road cut through what became a claustrophobic tunnel of emerald.

Samuel clutched an automatic assault rifle to his chest and stared down the barrel as if desensitizing himself to the concept of death. "They will not take this country. You know? It is ours. Our gods will not allow this to happen."

All Vasilij could think to do was nod. His palms were drenched with so much sweat he feared the weapon would slip from his hands, strike the floor, and accidentally kill someone. He tightened the strap around his shoulder and exhaled once.

Intermittent rattles swam through the peaceful baby blue sky. No screams, no voices—just bullets. They were to join with another group of volunteers that made up the Slovenian Territorial Militia within minutes. He hadn't heard of anybody dying yet, though the skirmishes were increasing and the attacks on Slovenian property were becoming more frequent. A man who called himself Vasilij's captain told his ragtag team about a weapons depot being compromised not too far away and how the explosion demolished any surrounding architecture.

The thought of a war being so close to home stunned his heart. He glanced at his brother, offered a confident smile, and rolled his shoulders back with a puffed chest that would've fooled any of the other civilian-turned-militant proudly wearing a jacket twice their size, whose rifle straps were twisted and loose, whose bootlaces were loose or dragging.

Vasilij and his brother were shoved off the bus single-file, which, to him, felt like they could easily be killed by a single, well-timed bullet. He closed his eyes and braced himself when he departed. His sole order was to stand guard at the threshold of his two ancestral homelands, point the barrel away from his allies, and fire upon the Yugoslavs whenever they showed their faces.

So, he did.

Blue-gray steel pockmarked with age and battles-past rolled into view. A solid, meter-long barrel trained on him and his brother. Before the tank could fire, the pathetic rattling of gunfire preceded the earth-shaking *boom!* that followed.

A fool's war—a joke of a battle. The Ten-Day War was made the subject of underhanded comments uttered by drunkards at taverns and bars. "They saw us," one tipsy man said years after the war ended. "And they turned heels, like scared dogs—tails between their legs! Shit hanging out of their ass! Gone, gone, gone!"

Concrete splintered when the tank fired shell number one, its impact casting an opaque plume of smoke and debris high into the sky, enough to block the sun and blind his allies.

"We had God on our side that day, boys!"

Vasilij saw a face in the smoke. It took the form of a serpent, laughing, mouth agape and jaw detached.

"Scared those Yugoslavs back to their ugly mothers!"

The face contorted two more times until he could peer into the thick, gray veil of ashen mist that proliferated throughout the severed border. A form effortlessly swam through, its arms outstretched and bent in terrible angles. He heard his brother's choked voice to his immediate right. "Vasilij!"

"Samuel!" he shouted before pushing himself away from the ground, coughing up black and swaying in space. The grinding of metal against asphalt grew louder, and so did the sound of rifles that splintered shells from their insignificant barrels.

Vasilij clutched his Samuel's hand through the dying fog and they laced their quaking fingers together. He watched as his brother's rifle bounced against his hip, idle and cold, and finally thanked the gods he had never believed in.

Samuel asked, "Did you see her? Did you see her?"

"Who? Samuel, who?"

Vasilij caught his brother's falling weight and tripped over split concrete. He landed on his back and smacked his unprotected head against the hard ground. Samuel's lingered inches from his, but he could not detect his breath.

Slovenia won the war on the same day as Samuel's funeral.

7

Vasilij was an old man with a weak heart and a dull mind in May of 2023.

This woman, Jenny, a stranger with a heart of silver, portrayed the same ignorant and lifeless expression Samuel held when he died. It's as if she knew his past and chose to mock Vasilij to his very face.

Her tongue lolled, her eyes soft and damp. She draped over him like a wet blanket. Her limp head locked between Vasilij's right cheek and the groove of the same shoulder. While his heart raced, hers slowed. Each one of Jenny's faculties careened to silence as though they were overhead lights in a freshly decommissioned hospital wing. A portion of his torso wetted with her blood, and snot painted his upper lip with a glossy sheen.

Vasilij only shifted from stillness to nudge Jenny's corpse so he could breathe a little better. With the dense fog continuing to eat away his vision, there wasn't a better place to be than on the ground with the ability to see every angle, to parse through the terrible cloud and determine where the attacker could be, where he could go.

He's still nearby. He must be.

Hot tears rolled down Vasilij's round cheeks, its salt staining the corners of his mouth with a flavor that catapulted him thirty-two years in the past.

Why am I alive? Why is he keeping me alive?

His eyes adjusted to the mist as if his mind were a radio tuning to another station. Within the white sea swam an impossibly tall figure. Its energy was feminine and electric, its gait drifted swiftly and steady. With every second that passed while watching the entity, his lungs strained from holding his breath, and by the time it disappeared, his ears were thrumming.

Vasilij released a slow, cathartic exhale.

A quiet prayer decorated the empty space. He repeated a mantra to comfort himself. His lips were inches from Jenny's ear. In his native tongue, he muttered, "I am alive. I am strong. I have no fear."

He wanted her to wake up.

"We're alive. We're strong. We—*we* have no fear."

Viscous blood trailed through her unscented red-brown hair and knotted locks along the way. He could feel its warmth crawl over his face. His lower lip shuddered, and he turned away with urgency prodding his muscles.

A recognizable numbness dulled his nerves. The limp body of Jenny slumped to the side as he excavated himself from her embrace. The impulse to apologize nagged at him, so he did. With a slightly bent knee, he opened his mouth to recite the same prayer offered to his brother. No sounds emerged from his tight throat.

A male voice barked from behind him in Slovenian. "You're a monster!"

Vasilij's spine stiffened. He turned to the stranger with hot tears burrowing canals through the blood caked onto his face. "No! Listen! This wasn't me! I-I didn't do this!" He stretched both hands in front of him and approached the newcomer with a quaking lower lip. "Please believe me. Someone else did this!"

A young man with a short crop of wild, dark curls timidly approached Jenny's body. He wore a tight, black hoodie meant for someone smaller than him. The stranger crouched and touched his forefingers to her neck. After gesturing to the gaping hole that crumbled the back of her skull, he said, "You're sick. You killed her!"

"*No!*" Vasilij clumsily answered through a harsh scoff. "Her attacker is still here. It's not me, it's not me!" He checked behind his shoulder, almost ducking with expectation of another incoming attack. "Please, you must believe me! We were friends!"

"Friends, huh?" the young man said with a sharp exhale. He stood with ease and reached into his pocket before revealing an aging cell phone. "Sure. I believe you, but as you know, it's ultimately up to the police to decide who's at fault."

"It's useless. The phones don't work here. It won't work."

He flashed the small screen and shrugged; the call successfully connected to Wi-Fi network he hadn't seen before.

Vasilij's brow furrowed. He eyed Jenny's makeshift weapon lying under her, its splintered end breaching from under her armpit. When his gaze checked back in on the stranger, their eyes met, and he felt a strong pulse of fear in his throat.

He nodded to the obscured object. "Is that the weapon? The one used to kill her?"

"I did *not* hurt her."

"No? It seems like you really want it. Is there evidence? Maybe your fingerprints, or her blood?" He held the device to his ear. "Hello? Can you hear me? Yes, sir, I can hear you just fine."

Vasilij's face stretched as his jaw dropped. "You're lying to me. There's no one on the line. No one is talking to you."

"Yes, I'd like to report a murder. I'm staying at the *Crossroads—*"

"—you're *lying*!" Vasilij launched himself and swiped the phone out of the stranger's hand.

With a shout that flayed the otherwise peaceful ambiance, the stranger sank into a defensive pose and raised a balled fist. "You asshole! You shit!" One failed punch, sidestepped by Vasilij, was all the stranger could muster before a teal flash tackled him to the floor. The young man ended up mere inches from Jenny's face with his own pressed against the hardwood.

One of Christopher's hands wrapped around the stranger's wrists and the other kept a firm press against the back of his head. Shouting in English, "You like hurting people, brother? *Huh*?" The rough edge of his accent rounded each syllable and strands of spit tangled in the man's curly mane.

Vasilij stood to the side, feckless and immobile, with trembling hands and one eye still glued to the wooden weapon. After struggling to find the courage to speak, he shouted, "You okay?" Christopher didn't look away from the stranger. The intensity splayed on his face read to Vasilij as dire. "Um... Um... Oh, uh—Pennie?"

The name weakened Christopher as if a breaker had suddenly been flipped off. This afforded the young stranger a chance to wriggle free, but Christopher regained his cognizance long enough to muster up the decision to punch the man's skull.

It bounced against the floor and a hissing seethe followed a pained groan. Christopher spat, "Dodgy fucker. *Don't get up!* What'd you say, mate?" He waited for a response from Vasilij, but an empty expression wandered onto his face instead—the primary symptom of a language barrier. "Fuck's sake. What'd you say about Pennie, mate?"

He lowered his brow and gestured around the room as if to say *where is she?*
Christopher clued into Vasilij's intentions after he performed a confused shrug. "She's hurt bad, bro." His dry tongue plodded against the inside of his dry mouth. "*This* asshole was in our room. The... Our window was broken, a-and—why the hell am I even explaining this to you? You don't understand one goddamned thing I'm saying, do you?"

Vasilij sensed the teal man's frustrations and apologized under his breath. While his ally continued his distressed rant, Vasilij returned to Jenny's body with a stiff crouch. In the corner of his eye, there was a minor ebb of struggle from the others. His shaky hands probed Jenny's pockets. A nauseated grimace flowered.

"Ew, mate. The hell are you doing?"

Vasilij's response was both dry and lost on the English boy. "Her key. I think we should hold onto it." He respectfully pulled away long enough to offer a pantomimed gesture; his wrist turned as though twisting a doorknob.

"I really should've stuck to Duolingo. Fuck me. Aren't you going to do something a little more useful, like, I don't know, call the police? *Policija?*"

The Slovene man paired a brusque eye roll with a scoff. His excavation of Jenny's pockets supplied him with a crumpled fast-food receipt and a pocket-sized notebook.

"Can you help me here, mate?" Christopher called.

Vasilij flipped through the pages and felt a grin crawl over his creased face. "My name is Vasilij," he said with some effort and a hard rounding of the vowels. "Where is the... Library?" He never would've taken Jenny for a reader.

"Are you having a laugh? Mate! *Vasilij!*"

Christopher's shift in tone spawned an apologetic frown from the distracted Vasilij. He flipped through a few more pages before landing on a section labeled *verbs*. "I will help you."

"Glad to hear it."

He hunched over and inched his hand toward Jenny's weapon. "I'll make sure you aren't forgotten," he said while dragging the chair leg from under her lifeless body.

Both Vasilij and Christopher shared a thin second where the world froze. Their undivided attention might have been enough of an offering to watch her body spring back to life.

She remained prone, folded.

Christopher increased his grip around the stranger's wrists. "Big man, yeah? Let me see your face. Yo, Vazzy!"

"Y-yes?"

"Ask him why he hurt my girlfriend. Go on. Translate for me!" His wild head bobs only further confused the Slovene man. "Ask him about Pennie!"

Vasilij swallowed hard, pouted, and asked the stranger, "Can you understand him?"

The young man hissed, "I don't *want* to understand him. He's a fucking plague. Him and the rest of them—especially that Western whore he fucks."

Christopher's head spun. "What did he say? Is he talking about Pennie?"

Vasilij ignored his newfound ally; he couldn't see himself having another chance to dig deeper. "Did you hurt her?" The stranger bared his teeth like a hound in one of the countless portraits stashed around the building. A half-second ticked by before he added, "Why? Why are you hurting people?"

The stranger pressed his lips into a thin line that made his already hairless face younger.

"Fuck this." Christopher coerced him by twisting both of his bony wrists to an uncomfortable angle. He proceeded, slowly and surgical, until the assailant's bones creaked.

Vasilij's eyes closed, the scene too much for his empathetic soul. "Just answer him. Seems he's the type to kill someone who crosses him."

"Oh, yeah? Well, fuck him." he shouted before calling Christopher a terrible slur based off of his melanated skin.

Vasilij drew in a slow inhale and tasted the damp air on his tongue. Mist blanched the scene as if they were floating on a wooden raft atop a warm, endless ocean. He could hardly make out the full form of Christopher and they were only feet apart. "If I tell him what you said, he'll crush your skull."

"You share his language? That's disgusting."

"Can you at least tell me about the fog? I can negotiate your release if—"

"Take my advice and rid your tongue of that cancer."

"Is there a machine? You're using the fog to attack people. Did you do this? Is there a machine, or—or is the building made of traps? Are Sabiha and Romeo involved?"

A dribbling laughter fell from the stranger's lips.

Christopher shot a hot glance at his new ally. "He's bullshitting us, isn't he? You're just straight up bullshitting us. Where'd you come from, you straight piece of filth?" He dug his knee into the young man's lower spine and delighted as the assailant feebly fought back. "You're trying to death roll me! Like a goddamned crocodile. Vazzy? Get down here, help me out. Come on, pick up the pace."

Understanding the word *help* sandwiched between other nonsense, Vasilij read the situation and pressed the chair leg flat against the back of the stranger's neck. This worked better than he thought, as it kept him in a consistent chokehold. Whenever the young man started to cough, he lightened his grip.

He re-added pressure ad hoc.

Christopher marveled at the clever, almost brutal way Vasilij kept the stranger inundated. "You've got a dark streak, ain't you, Vazzy?"

"Search his pockets."

"Eh?"

Vasilij used one hand to quickly pat his own pockets.

Christopher took the cue and searched the stranger's black hoodie for items of interest. "Let's see. Who the hell are you? You must have a license, a phone—*something*... I'll

91

call the *policija* as soon as the phones work again. You hear that, mate? *Policija!* You're going to piss yourself when... Ah, what's this?" He recovered a heavy set of keys from the frontmost pouch of the stranger's hoodie.

As soon Christopher extracted his keyring, the stranger thrashed and shouted profanities in his native tongue.

"Could you help me out here, Vazzy?"

Vasilij straightened his perpetually curved spine, adjusted his consistently aching knees, and leaned down with considerably more force. Splintered wood bit into the stranger's skin as it rolled over the nape of his neck. This act suffocated the young man, and he quickly rose into a panic.

A weak string of staccato breath filtered into the stranger's throat, and a swarm of molten hornets crashed into the interior of his throbbing skull. Feeling a twinge of guilt, Vasilij released some pressure. The young man erupted into a violent coughing fit.

"Wow! Look at these," Christopher said, impressed by the collection of polished nickel keys. He held up the collection and jangled them in front of the stranger's face. "You're quite the busy man."

But the assailant didn't stop coughing. His chest heaved as he drew in choked breath. His cheeks were painted pink and sweat formed on his pasty face.

Christopher exchanged a look with Vasilij before removing his knee from the stranger's back. He shushed him. "Christ, you're a baby. Well, maybe this is what you get." As he spoke, his confidence swandived. "Karma. S-something like that."

Vasilij spoke to his ally with fear lacing around each word. In his mother tongue, "He's just a kid. He probably goes to university. This isn't good. No, no. This isn't right."

The babble from his Slovene ally only increased Christopher's anxiety. "A-alright, just—calm down, bro. Watch him, okay?" Christopher dropped the keyring into the front pocket of his teal jacket and stood to his feet.

Vasilij hovered nearby, the chair leg still trained in his sweaty grip.

"I'm not trying to murder someone today. Mm-mm. Your death ain't up to me. Stop coughing! No, you're never gonna find me trapped in some spooky fucking jail cell eating goddamned *borscht*. Fucking Slovenia, man. Will you shut the fuck up?"

The young man rolled to his back, clutched his throat, and performed a handful of strained gags before rolling to his knees. A curtain of loose coils obscured his pale face. The trembling hand that wiped spit away from his glossy lips was the same hand that drew a bloody shard of glass from his waistband.

With dizzying clumsiness, the assailant galloped forward while using his free hand to brace the ground. He swung the shiv upward and punctured the center of Christopher's gut. The glass easily tore through the teal jacket and dyed it a sickly, dark violet. He applied a consistent twisting motion while digging through either front pocket of the jacket with his free hand.

Christopher ground his teeth until they were dust. His large hands wrapped over his attacker's head and squeezed with gradually diminishing pressure; as his life-force drained away, so did his strength.

The attacker freed himself, tensed the already tormented expression on his face, and prepared to plunge a final blow into Christopher's wide chest. He changed tactics when the heavy footfall from Vasilij's work boots alerted him of his imminent arrival. He ducked to the right, coughed twice when his over-exerted lungs panged from stress, and hastily prepared a key to room six, the nearest refuge.

Vasilij hesitated between tracking the assailant and rescuing the tourist.

Christopher lowered himself to the wooden floor. Both hands clutched his seeping wound. "Fuck it," he shouted with breath softening each syllable. "Kill that son of a bitch."

Autonomy took over Vasilij's body as if he were remote controlled by demon in Hell. Someone else controlled each lunging step, every steady exhale. Jenny's weapon tightened in his grip, and he hugged the object against his chest as though he were a young soldier once again.

The door to room six cracked open and Vasilij yelled for anyone inside to hide. The stranger's black hoodie melted into the sickly orange glow of an overhead sconce. A mouth opened to swallow the young man, and its teeth urgently gnashed to take a bite...

8

...but was denied its seal by the splintered chair leg.

The door bounced open with a rubbery *thwup-pup-bub-bub* and Vasilij shouldered his way into room six with either bare hand arched outwards. His attention sharpened as he probed each inch of the room. Between his heartbeat endlessly dribbling in his head and his eyes that refused to quit shuddering, it became difficult for him to focus.

The mist started to diffuse. He spotted the assailant's clear silhouette approaching the terracotta curtains every room shared and shouted at him to stop.

To his surprise, the assailant obeyed him.

Vasilij inspected a nasty wound carved in the young man's hand, presumably from having gripped the glass shiv used to fell Christopher.

The murderer rotated on the heels of his off-white sneakers and said, "You don't have to join them, brother," his rasped voice insisted in Slovenian. It visibly pained him to speak. "Why sacrifice yourself for the sake of some godless Westerners?"

He took a half-step forward. "Why are you doing this?"

"Because it must be done, and someone has to do it." The stranger glowered at Vasilij while nursing his wound; he kept pressure on his hand by pressing it against his chest. "Maybe you'll stop chasing me if I tell you that you're not part of the plan. Stop walking."

Vasilij slowed to a stop. By a quick calculation, he couldn't have been more than ten paces from the assailant. Their conversation had been lubricated, and the information he desperately wanted flowed with ease. "What do you mean by—"

A feeble voice squawked from Vasilij's right: "Please leave!" An elderly woman had been sitting upright in her bed with a thin comforter drawn to her neck. She observed the confusing scene with a remarkably pale face. In a language neither of the men understood, she said, "I do not need room service at five in the morning, thank you very much!"

He watched gears turn behind the stranger's eyes as his gaze flitted from Vasilij to the old woman. The top layer of an onion had been stripped away, and its vulnerable bulb remained; the man's deft ability to switch personalities whiplashed Vasilij as he idly stood by and watched the murderer stumble to her bed.

"Please!" the young man cried in English with the ostensible hope that the woman shared the language.

She recoiled when he showed her his wound. "Oh, dear. Is that blood? That's not good."

"Help me!"

Vasilij's eyes widened in disbelief. He scoffed. "You reject their ways yet ask for their help?"

The stranger abused the only English phrase he knew until irritation battered the old woman. "Help me, please! Help!"

She dry swallowed and twisted her face from empathy to annoyance. "Yes, yes. What is it you need?"

"Please!" he shook his injured hand to exaggerate his pain.

"What do you want from me? Do you need a bandage? A hug?" She hiked her shoulders. "Do you need me to call your mum?" Her attention briefly turned to Vasilij, who had pulled the phrase book from his pocket. "You're so bored, you're reading?"

Vasilij's fingers acted as bookmarks as he quickly transitioned from one page to another. "He... Is... Not good." He looked up to the old woman for approval.

Silence stagnated between the three, and even though he spoke very limited English, the stranger awaited her reply with bated breath.

"Well, obviously not. He's got blood all over the place. The sheets, too. I'm not paying for this, if they ask. It's not my blood." She huffed. "I shouldn't have to pay if it's not my blood."

The young man found the situation just as frustrating as she had. When he stepped away from the bed, his foot bumped into a hard suitcase lying against the wooden frame. His nostrils flared as he stared at it.

Vasilij could see the gears turning once again. His mouth parched. "Don't hurt her," he demanded. Both hands stretched outright as though he were a wrestler preparing to grapple with his opponent.

"It would be easy," the stranger replied with a half-wink. "She's made of parchment paper and glass."

For the second time in his life, Vasilij saw red. It appeared as a subtle vignette that crept into his peripherals, remaining only when he ruminated over the young man's cruel statement. He calmly said, "Listen, kid. There's something about myself I'm proud of. It's difficult to convince me of violence."

"Oh?" His knees slowly bent like a pair of birch trees surrendering to the whim of a windstorm.

"It wasn't until the war was brought to my doorstep that I ever considered killing another man." Vasilij gradually leaned into his next step. "As you stand before me right now, I don't see a child who deserves a slap on the wrist." His heel pressed against the floor without a sound.

A wild grin grew on the stranger's face. In the corner of his eye, he made out the elderly woman stare on as though she found herself trapped in a morbid theater production. "What do you see, then, old man?"

"You are the war, and this place is my doorstep." The floorboard creaked when he walked towards him.

The stranger's face blanched, and his breathing quickened. An expression of agony mutated into flared nostrils, shown teeth, and a tensed jaw. Vasilij's gaze soared through the thick fog to connect with the elderly woman's eyes.

Before she could blink or look away, Vasilij trickled two English words from his down-curved mouth: "No friend."

The young man snatched the suitcase and twisted his torso with a pained grunt. He thrusted the heavy object into the window. His first strike ended up being a remarkable success; the sound of glass crunched from behind the veil of a red-orange curtain and the woman shrieked.

Vasilij shouted, "You're a coward if you run!" He wandered forward with his heart in his throat. Every beat caused his eyesight to pulse.

Another strike, and a sheet of glass crumbled to the floor. The stranger shook away a collection of crystalline shards from his sneakers before turning to face the incoming

Vasilij. A smirk coiled on his face, his thin lips contorting with pride. "Fuck"—he heaved the large suitcase into Vasilij's chest—"*you!*"

Vasilij tumbled backward, coughed out what little air remained in his lungs, and collapsed to his back while the old woman sobbed into her shaking hands.

When the red seeped away and his awareness returned, he looked to the broken window and cursed. The stranger had vaulted himself over the threshold and disappeared into an adjacent room. He shoved the suitcase away from him and slammed the floor with a balled fist.

His head spun and his lungs desperately grabbed at the thick air to replenish its oxygen reserves. He listened to the awful song of an old woman crying as he stared at the unimpressive ceiling.

Vasilij squeezed his eyes shut and gritted his teeth. A hot tear fell and its dewy tail wrapped around his round cheek. He caught himself thinking about what he could've done, what he should've done and replayed only half of the memory before being shaken back to reality by the woman's croaking voice. "Oh, great," she said. "*Another* visitor."

A familiar voice choked out from behind Vasilij. "Room f-five." Christopher, out of breath, leaned against the far wall and held up five bloody fingers. He transformed his splayed hand into a single pointer finger and jabbed at the air to reference the broken window.

"Five. *Pet!* Okay, yes." Vasilij allowed himself another long moment to fully recover from the assault. He leaned forward and smacked his cheeks several times to keep the adrenaline flowing.

The elderly woman squinted and gasped. She asked Christopher in a delicate accent if it had been Vasilij who hurt him.

"N-no, ma'am. It was the hoodie lad. H-he slashed my girlfriend's leg." Christopher replied weakly and slid to the floor. "Got me good. Killed a lady n-named Jenny, too. Vazzy's friend."

Vasilij used the woman's bed frame to lift himself upright. He spoke to Christopher in Slovenian with ardency stiffening his tone. "I'll find him. Okay? Next time, I won't hesitate."

Christopher's voice turned airy, and his lips dried before Vasilij's eyes. His face had become the color of ash. "I-I really wish I could understand you, mate. Hey, Vazzy, do me a favor? Promise me th-that Pennie will be okay."

"Pennie. Yes." The image of the bleeding man blurred behind a curtain of warm tears.

"Room two." Christopher lifted his fingers to show a V-shape. He groaned and cinched his eyes. Deep lines etched onto his forehead and beads of sweat were caught in each fold as if they were dams desperately preventing an incoming flood. When he relaxed, dew resumed traveling until his bushy eyebrows caught them like rain against a forest canopy. His hand fell limp.

The old woman asked through frayed nerves, "Is he okay?"

A thick swallow dripped down Christopher's throat. "Oh, yeah. I'm f-fine." The same breath used to speak his final words dragged all the air from his strained lungs. His head rolled to the side with his mouth cracked open. Both hands clutched the deep perforation that ruined his teal designer jacket.

Vasilij crawled toward him with his jaw agape. "No—*no.* Christopher?" He shook the leg of his acquaintance. Denied a response, the man turned to the old woman who offered her own grief by huffing out loud, bed-shaking sobs; each dry cough usurped the quiet ambiance of room six, but the sound of crinkling glass stole the attention of both of its denizens.

Two hands, skinny and crooked, pulled apart the curtains that struggled against the ancient rods. A red-headed woman with a long face and bright makeup poked her head into the room. An expression of great concern had been worn in sorrow. She adjusted her glasses to make out the pair of grieving individuals. "Sorry if I'm—oh, my. Oh, God, no."

The elderly woman asked a question in a language that certainly wasn't English. The way each syllable line-danced with the other in fat, square movements reminded him of German.

Anna introduced herself in her primary tongue, and the old woman sighed in relief before replying in the same language. "My name is Rene. I wish I could say it's nice to meet you, but I'm not completely certain I'm awake right now! What a nightmare I've found myself in."

"Unfortunately, you're as awake as I am. That man in the black hoodie—he's not a good person."

Rene's bottom lip plumed when she looked at the idle body of Christopher. Before she could verbalize one of the hundreds of thoughts running through her mind, Anna tilted her head downward and cursed under her breath.

"I-I should've done something. I heard somebody screaming next door, so I hid under the bed like the coward I am. I should've"—she clenched both fists and examined her neighbor's room in a panic—"found a *weapon* instead of being so absolutely useless!"

"Now, don't you say that!" Rene said as she peeled both covers away. "Don't torture yourself with 'could haves' and 'would haves'. Especially now, when there's so much sadness in the air. Dear, it was *I* who was screaming. Talk about a coward—I'm the definition! But we must remain strong. A psychopath is on the loose and two is two too many casualties."

"Two?"

"Yes. Our dear Christopher, if I heard right, and a poor woman named Jenny."

The room crumbled around Anna as though she were falling through the Earth and entering the vacuum of space. In a voice so quiet, her words sounded like raindrops against asphalt, "Jenny is dead?" She swallowed hard and checked on Vasilij, who hadn't moved from Christopher's side.

"That's what he said, at least. The dead one—not the Slovenian one."

Anna pulled away from the window and let the curtain fall back into place. For the time being, she needed privacy. Having already locked her door behind the stranger, she felt secure enough to pace along a short path while fighting back sobs.

When she returned, the first thing she said was, "I'm useless."

Rene's legs were thrown over the side of the bed. She couldn't extract herself from the only place she felt safe.

Curtains hugged Anna's head as it hung in the window's frame. Her eyes cast to the ground to count each minuscule shard of glass. She leaned forward with her knobby elbows.

Rene's bony fingers played with one another while losing herself to thought. She intoned, "What a mess. Despite everything, I still feel terrible for the owners of the place. All the glass and the blood... Are you alright, dear?" No response from the red-headed woman. Rene drew in a deep breath, stretched her fragile arms, and lifted away from the bed.

Anna turned her gaze to the old woman and performed a soft, obligatory smile. She batted the moisture away from her lashes. "Sorry. I just don't know what to do."

"Let's start with this: it's a pleasure to meet you." She stuck her small, wrinkled hand out.

Anna flexed her nostrils and temporarily swallowed her sadness. She pulled the curtains aside and reciprocated the handshake. "Likewise."

"It's relieving to find someone of the same *lingua franca* so far from home. I have questions if you have answers."

"I can try, Miss Rene."

"Good. Our friend..." They both oriented their attention to Vasilij, who remained in stasis, cross-legged and only inches away from Christopher's body. "It's evident he's going through a crisis and, while it breaks my heart, I'm entirely uncertain of his motives. Can we trust him? They argued with one another in the same language. Do we assume they know each other? If so, are they allies or enemies?"

Anna frowned. She replied only after it became evident Rene wanted her to. She internally battled with competing imagery of Christopher's corpse and her imagination of Jenny's. "I can't see how they would know each other. The age difference, for one."

"That's fair. All this thinking! I need a coffee, then I'll put on my Sherlock cap."

"I'm not sure room service is available right now, Miss Rene."

Rene brushed shards of glass away from her path with her naked toes. In a whisper, she asked, "Do you feel comfortable with him? He's just *staring* at the dead boy, and it's become quite creepy."

Anna seriously considered the question. She observed Vasilij's slumped posture, his hanging head. "Perhaps we should leave him be. There's enough trauma to go around. There's no reason to indulge in his."

"Yes, but—oh, goodness. My door's still open," Rene's nostrils flared. "I don't want that lunatic coming back in." She cleared her throat and switched to English. "Sir? Excuse me?"

Vasilij gently stirred but didn't answer.

"Could you shut the door?" No luck. To Anna, in German: "My dear, you were smart enough to lock your door?"
"Yes, of course. As soon as he left."

Rene called for Vasilij once more before giving up with a scoff. "It probably doesn't matter, anyway."

Anna tilted her head. "What do you mean?"
"That man managed to unlock mine, didn't he?"

Anna rested her hands on the window frame and winced at receiving the sting of a jagged edge. "Shit. Wait, what do you mean?"

She leaned against the wall and skewed a frown. "Unless my memory is worse than I thought, I'm quite confident I locked my door last night." The old woman used the bedframe and the wall to negotiate around the broken glass.

"Careful, Miss Rene. Are you saying he has the key to your room?"

Rene waddled past Vasilij with her straw-like legs while saying, "He had a keyring on him. Stuffed it back into his pocket right after he broke in. It seems he could open every door in this building if he wanted to." She exerted a small push—one strong enough to close the door, yet gentle enough to do so without making a sound. She latched the lock. "You know, with how young he is, he could be the owners' son."

A drapery of sweat fell over Anna like a heated blanket. It coated her skin with discomfort and summoned sweat across her brow. "That... Complicates things."

"Does it?" Rene replied after sitting on the edge of the bed. The short journey winded her, and she wiped fresh exhaustion from her eyes. "This fog is quite annoying." She attempted to wave away the mist with a wagging hand.

"Yes, I agree," Anna inspected the sill with disquiet taming her voice. She used the curtain to clear off the wood. "It's a whole thing. The fog, I mean."

"Go on, then. Give me something! Even a crumb of information would be nice. Oh, crumb cake would be lovely with a nice coffee."

"I suppose it is fairly important to know. There we go." She brushed a thumb across the cleared sill and stuck it out with pride.

Rene pouted and looked at the cold body of Christopher idle in the corner of her room. "Go on, then. Distract me from my caffeine migraine—among other things."

"Not only does the fog obfuscate things, but it twists them around. It turned the building into a maze. These windows shouldn't be connected, you see?"

Rene blinked away a stinging sensation in her eyes. "I was curious about that."

"And the staircase is missing. It just vanished!"

The old woman contemplated this for a moment. "Mm. Does this mean we can't get to the kitchen?"

"Priorities, Miss Rene!"

"Yes, yes. I know."

Vasilij tossed a weighted exhale from between his lips, which simultaneously startled the two women; the sensation had started to crawl its way up his esophagus the moment life drifted from Christopher's eyes. He stood up and gave the body another sorrowful glance before unlocking the door.

Anna hissed at him to stay inside. "Please stay here," she said. "It's not a good idea to leave."

Vasilij loosely shook his head and said, "I have to find Pennie." He exited after arming himself with Jenny's weapon.

"What'd he say?" Rene asked, and Anna shrugged.

9

The distinct sound of scraping brass let Vasilij know someone had locked the door behind him.

An ocean of fog spread before him, somehow thicker than before, stifling the already dull points of illumination that belonged to the sparingly mounted sconces. Somewhere within its icy grasp happened to be the body of a brave woman, of a new and short-lived friend.

Vasilij checked the number of the room he just left. "*Šest*. Okay." He pointed the splintered weapon in front of him as if it were a dowsing rod and trailed the wall to gather his bearings until he came across another door. "*Štiri*." One more door and he'd reach room two where the wounded Pennie should be.

Spikes of heightened awareness jettisoned around him like ejections from the sun, reaching and disintegrating erratically, intending to act as an alarm if he came across another dark shadow swimming through the mist. *Nobody should be out here*, he thought, just as he reached room two. *I should also not be out here.*

The stiff knob didn't move. He seethed and tapped the door with his weapon. "Pennie?"

No answer.

Vasilij debated knocking any further, his hackles were already up. Behind him would be the door to room one and his subconscious nagged at him to think critically of the situation before questing forth.

The short wade filled an invisible panic meter to the brim and Vasilij filled with equal parts relief and disdain when he failed to open room one as well.

Vasilij stood at the precipice of the missing stairwell and looked down at the neat rows of planks. He spent a few moments inspecting the flooring and marveled at the seamless transition from one plank to another; no mechanisms, no glue could be identified. A door creaked open somewhere in the hallway and he clenched the weapon, gritted his teeth, and turned to face the abyss.

An image of Jenny's peaceful face scarred the interior of his busy mind, how her eyes remained locked open and observant, how she may have heard, saw, processed every event thereafter. The very idea burned his spirit and guided his feet.

Silence pressed onto him like a heavy coat and a high-pitched whine tuned in his right ear, as if his internal voice had instead switched into an old radio. He shook off an encroaching feeling of terror and mentally counted his breaths; Vasilij wouldn't stop marching until he ended up face-to-face with the hooded man. His conscience begged him not to resort to violence, and every time that small voice spoke up, he bombarded it with a series of graphic images involving Jenny, Christopher, and what his wild imagination drew up for Pennie.

Cradling the insignificant weapon reminded Vasilij an awful lot of how it felt to wield an automatic assault rifle.

Three decades after the fact, Vasilij reconciled with his cowardice during the Ten-Day War. He relied on his brother's bravado as the model for confidence he sorely lacked. Only days in had Samuel been killed, but their beautiful country remained the backdrop of a terrible battle that lasted another week.

By the time a ceasefire was established, he had only spent three bullets from the magazine he had difficulty locking into place. All three of his shots missed their targets, and he thanked God every single day that the remittance of such karma never touched his soul.

These thoughts distracted him long enough for him to scale the entire length of the hallway in what felt like a blink of an eye. Vasilij tossed a glance behind his shoulder and wondered if he passed Jenny's corpse or if it had been recovered by a passerby.

He met the window at the end of the long stretch and frowned at the strange image: thread bound the curtains together, the fabric had been stapled to the wood. Before he could waste time devising another asinine theory, the splintered chair leg found itself embedded in the fabric.

Vasilij grunted as he tore downward, then pulled back the splintered piece of wood and attacked again...

...and again, and again, until the curtain snatched against his improvised tool and yanked away from the rod. The clattering of light metal paired with heavy breaths from the irate Vasilij who wanted nothing more than to catch a swallow of fresh air with the understanding that it could be his last.

The woods were unaffected by the strange magic that proliferated through the building. He leaned forward and inspected the mulch-laden parking lot with a furrowed brow. He gazed into the expanse of woods where a calm stream broke through the trees.

Just beyond the cold glass was freedom. As far as he could tell, the outside world was exempt from the rules twisting the reality of the cozy abattoir he'd been trapped in.

The back of his neck tickled as if being caressed by a wight. He swallowed his breath and twisted volte-face to observe the hallway. With how thick the fog became and how much stress panged in his tired skull, he could've easily mistaken a short bout of movement as an optical illusion. He prepared his weapon, but the longer he stared into the abyss, the less danger he felt.

Nobody rushed him. He didn't hear footfall nor the shuffling of clothes. The straight hallway turned into a silent maze of improbability; the monster who murdered Jenny and Christopher could've been anywhere.

Twelve cramped rooms, each of them containing the bare minimum, all of them woven together in a para-natural tapestry that bound the souls of each inhabitant. Somewhere in this building—whether it was five, fifteen, or fifty feet away—was the most dangerous man he'd ever encountered, and it truly appeared that he had mastered all the rules of this new reality.

Vasilij picked up his pace and tried the handle of each door along the way. Each one had been locked by someone, and by the time he made his way back to the opposite side of the hallway, heavy panting fell from his cracked lips. A door slammed farther into the mist, and the sound of a dragged object captured his interest.

He clutched his weapon and jogged forward. The idea of following a straight path was laughable. Another door slammed and the subsequent rattling of keys meant the killer, once again, remained just out of reach as though the murderer had mastered the building's new laws—like he had a map marked with X's and O's.

Vasilij spun on his heels, readied his weapon, and breathed through his gaped lips.

The muffled voice of a woman rose in intensity before exploding in a shout. He attempted to locate the new victim, but the thick, swirling fog deadened the sound. Moisture stung his widened eyes, and his chest heaved in a rising panic. Her scream seemed to linger in the air as though being captured by the mist like a polaroid.

He shuffled along the floor and snapped his focus to any new sound that alerted him; the crunching of soil underfoot, the scraping of heels along wooden planks, the frightful protest from what sounded like the red-headed woman.

Vasilij broke into a full sprint until he returned to the large window at the end of the hallway. If he shattered the fucking thing, he could easily jump out and tumble down into a patch of high grass—either that, or a series of wooden trellises and stakes that sprouted from the ground like wooden wrists and straight fingers reaching up to the dark sky.

A shrill pitch whirred in his ear. As if guided by the strong wince that succeeded the sound, he turned and took in the sight of suite twelve. It was the final room, innocently tucked across from the eleventh suite.

Room twelve had been completely unmarked. No plaque, no numbers. Someone designed the suite to be innocuous.

Vasilij hesitated before the door with his free hand outstretched. Both lips were dry and cracked, his throat completely sapped of moisture. The sound of a sliding latch paralyzed him, but he fought through the intense lag and lurched forward toward the corner.

The door swung open with haste. The wood paused less than an inch from bashing in Vasilij's bulbous nose. He held his breath and learned to cherish the eventual strain from his lungs. There was only the sound of soft footfall from...

Another vivid image seared into the crack of space before him: *off-white sneakers*.

He swallowed any more hesitation, prayed to whatever god wanted to hear him, and kneed the door away before charging with the chair leg arced overhead.

The vicious murderer wore the face of a young man; many of the soldiers that stormed Vasilij's country did the same.

As if possessed, the killer turned, flashed a snarl, and raised a rusted screwdriver to protect himself against the incoming bludgeon. The fucked-up game of rock-paper-scissors raged for a half-second. *Chair leg* won against *screwdriver*.

Once Vasilij followed through with his strike, the pathetic tool shot out of the killer's hand and clattered deep into the mist. Vasilij reeled back for another strike and squashed the small voice that asked him to reconsider his actions.

An old classmate of his had been charred to ashes from a Molotov cocktail. Every time a neighbor barbecues beef, Vasilij sprints to the bathroom to empty everything in his stomach.

The blunt edge of the soft wood cracked against the young man's skull.

Vasilij's mother's best friend was crushed by a tank as it rolled over the vehicle she hid in. Her innards became one with the upholstery in an unidentifiable marriage of scrap and goo.

One large gash opened across the killer's forehead when the object struck downward at an awkward but effective angle.

A hail of hollow points cleaved Uncle Beno at the knees. He lives as an alcoholic, forever scratching at the missing limbs while parked in front of a flickering CRT television.

Tags of flesh hung off the chair leg's jagged edge. He listened to the pained shout of the murderer and relished in it as though the howls were a sound bath in a monastery. Streaks of crimson dug into the boy's face. His right eye had become a deflated pouch hanging against the bridge of his cheek.

Both he and Samuel saw the entity their family deified swimming through a cloud of debris—a goddess of the hunt, a titan of dark magick. They glimpsed the holy deity frolic amongst the shrapnel, skate along the broken concrete.

Vasilij raised his weapon overhead and charged his next attack to be the final one.

"Y-you don't understand," the stranger whined in their common tongue as he crawled backwards with one hand loosely clutching his scarlet veiled face. "I-I have no choice! Fuck! Fuck!"

Vasilij swung before he could process the boy's words. The rounded edge of the chair leg smacked against the killer's temple—the stranger's mess of curls only providing so much protection—and the strike rendered him motionless.

The amount of adrenaline traveling through Vasilij's body ached his heart and impeded his breaths. He tossed the weapon to the ground, clutched his chest, and grabbed the still-open door to equalize him. His eyes trailed from the defeated murderer to the interior of the unmarked room twelve.

A cramped bedroom, just like any other he could've walked into, had been decorated with the matching corpses of Jenny and Christopher set in a spacious wire kennel. A pile of fabric containing a stained teal jacket, and a cream top were bundled in a laundry hamper tucked in the corner. The two had been stripped of their clothes, left naked, and posed with leather muzzles wrapped over either face. A long, beech wood chest lived next to the bed, its contents disturbing enough without confirmation.

Vasilij's eyes softened at the revelation. His shoulders dropped while his heart rediscovered its rhythm. A string of snot matched the trajectory of his swinging head. When he dropped to his knees, he noticed the fog thinned out significantly more within room twelve. He could see from one side of the room to the next without an issue.

Wooden totems and hand painted portraits of hounds decorated several hanging shelves. Creatures from the past, their souls indelibly fused to the property, watched out on the scene with unmoving eyes and stolid expressions of approval.

He immediately erected himself when the diminutive form of Anna called for his help.

"Oh, God! Help me, please!" she shouted in German, then again in English. A plush scrunchy had been unsuccessfully used as a gag. She leaned against the back wall, directly parallel to the door, and had watched the entirety of Vasilij's show with only a snowy veil to block the more caustic details. She could make out the man through the matrix of wire making up the dented kennel.

He snapped from his stupor and met up with the woman whose outfit had been reduced to a tan brassiere and black underwear. With shaking hands, he attempted to tear away the plastic zip tie that bound her wrists. Vasilij's movements were clumsy, and his sharp, square nails sometimes dug into her skin as he negotiated the binding. She breathlessly spoke to him in English, and, from the few words he could pick up, identified the first few sentences as a warning, then that of gratitude. He replied, "Okay, okay. You okay. You okay."

He could choose a more appropriate sentence to calm her down from Jenny's phrase book at a later time. In fact, when everything calmed down after the police apprehended the murderer, they could sit across from each other with cups of coffee and practice for the rest of his three-day stay.

Unfortunately for Anna, there were only two other English phrases available to him, and one involved a library.

Vasilij's frantic movements slowed to a crawl when her muscles tensed. He stopped completely when her voice dropped into a sustained whine. Someone, *something*, loomed behind him and her eyes were trained on it. With no weapon to his name, with very little strength left in his body, he spun around with a courageous shout and whipped his fist toward—

10

A Mastiff.

He blinked and retrieved his sent fist. "A dog?"

The dark hound was tall, imposing, and utterly quiet. It sat with perfect posture, with steady breaths, with intelligent eyes, and didn't so much as flinch at Vasilij's sudden movement.

Vasilij apologized to the beast twice—the second more for him since the thought of violence against animals sickened him.

The pace of his throbbing heart thrummed against his tired ribcage. The backdrop of fog dissipated over the next minute, and, in time, he could make out the idle body of the young murderer resting in the hallway. He wondered if the boy was just unconscious, if the melee had been effective enough to have ended him—if *he* was brutal enough to have ended him.

The dog *woofed* once and every cell in Vasilij's body undulated. Anna broke into a dry sob. Her bony chest heaved to reveal every little bone in her ribcage as it pressed against her thin, pink flesh. The canine swung its massive head to the cage and coldly observed the enmeshed bodies. A pearlescent string of saliva stretched from its mouth. Its gaze returned to Vasilij, barked again, and they both stood up from their seated position.

The beast loped all the way to the young murderer's body and sat next to its head. It split its attention between the corpse, Vasilij, and the empty hallway.

Anna struggled to free herself from the tightened zip tie. The plastic cut into her raw flesh and drew several pellets of blood. They tapped to the floor below. "I-I want to go home," she spat out. A blubbering cry obscured the rest of her words. "I..."

Vasilij reached out to comfort the woman and, once again, the hound projected a booming alert. His hand withdrew and coiled as if it were a dead vine shrinking to nothingness. In Slovenian, he shouted, "What do you want?!"

Another booming *woof*. It reminded him of the tanks that fired into his country, how each shot rattled the ground. Each time, his nerves frayed a little more. The hound dipped its nose to the bloodied corpse and emitted a low, guttural groan.

"Do you want me to... Do you want me to do *this*? As in... *all of this?*" Vasilij gestured to the naked corpses of his acquaintances. The dog responded by subtly shifting its posture; its thick tail slapped twice against the floor.

"Oh, my God," he said to himself. Then, to Anna in their shared language of English, "*What the fuck?*"

Anna scoffed a laugh before returning to her pulsing sobs.

Vasilij rubbed his eyes with the meat of his fists and faced the hound with resolution cemented in his heart. He swallowed what little moisture remained and approached the statuesque dog with an invisible hand tamping his overactive heart. He flinched when the hound stood up, but calmed once he witnessed its tail flailing in slow, wide berths.

He stared down the expansive hallway and squinted. Though the fog had filtered away, the building was still without a staircase. He couldn't escape, not without suffering the potential injury from a steep drop. Vasilij resigned to ask the beast, "Is this what you want from me?"

It didn't respond, but it kept wagging. *Thump, thump*.

"Y-you want him in the cage?" He shook his head, clasped a hand over his mouth, and felt the stubble as he dragged it down his face. His next actions were completed with little thought, pure autonomy.

Vasilij slid the fresh corpse into room twelve and dropped the body next to the kennel. He cast a shaky exhale from his trembling lungs and unzipped the hoodie. His hands traveled down the length of the jacket until his knuckles brushed against the bulge of keys hidden in the front pocket. The hound barked its next demand and Vasilij understood. Within minutes, the young man, with his horribly deformed face, had been angrily stuffed into the cage alongside Jenny and Christopher.

A low growl, then a series of deafening barks.

"What now? What do you want?!" Vasilij shouted at the beast while covering his ears.

Anna's voice piped up from the back wall. "It's... He wants..."

"Do you speak dog?!"

She mimed a cupped hand to her mouth. "A muzzle."

The hound ceased its booming calls and the tension in Vasilij's body gradually melted away. Deep breaths cascaded from his mouth in overlapping sighs. "Okay," he said in English. Miming the object by cupping a hand over his face, he repeated, "*Muz-zle*." Anna nodded, then directed him to the beech wood chest by pursing her lips.

"That's where Benji got the others from."

Vasilij frowned. He would rather communicate with the dog, for it at least seemed to understand Slovenian.

"Benji," she repeated with a quiver in her throat. Anna took a moment to compose herself. "His name. It's his—his name, his *ime*. Right? *Ime?*" Her lower lip shook, and she glanced at the young man's posed corpse. "Sorry. I didn't want to die at the hands of a stranger."

The woman's explanation fell flat. Vasilij hushed her with a few quick *okays* and drifted past the ever-alert hound. A brass lock had been popped open and Vasilij had no issues lifting the lid. Inside were colorful leads of peeling leather, knotted harnesses, and chain collars with sickeningly sharp prongs. He retrieved one muzzle and shook off a leash that statically clung to it. Speaking clearly and confidently, since the beast apparently understood his language, "This one? Does it matter?"

The hound replied by returning to a straight-backed sit.

Vasilij held his breath as he returned to the kennel entrance in a crouch. He leaned inside far enough to maneuver the muzzle around Benji's face with his hands shaking like the last two leaves clinging to the branch of a dead tree. Exiting the cage, he gasped for clean air and snorted back loose snot. "Shit! I-is that it?" he asked the dog. "Please. Is that all you need from me?"

Seconds drifted by without a response. With every tick of his internal clock passing by, desperation filled his chest. Anna's voice piped, "Um... *Oprostite?*"

He rolled his eyes, turned to her, and stared into the woman's sallow face. In unabashed Slovenian, he asked, "What? Do you want to fucking do it?"

"S-sorry. I think maybe... Lock the—" she mimed the best she could with what little mobility as her bound wrists allowed. "Lock the, erm, kennel. Lock the door!"

Vasilij dropped his head forward, his forehead against the grating of the cage, and allowed heretofore tamped agony to manifest as quick falling, salty tears that met his pouty lower lip. The hound's bark tore him from catharsis, and he repeatedly punched the cage until obvious dents ate into the wiring. "What—do—you—want—*now?*"

"Sir!" the woman behind him shouted. She drew her knees into her chest and attempted to scramble up the wall. "No! Oh, God. Sir! Please, you have to run! You have to run! Get away, get... You..." Anna pushed herself up the wall, sniveled, and repeated a muddied German phrase before disappearing into the attached bathroom with a loud whine. The door slammed, the lock rattled, and Vasilij sobered in an instant.

The fine, straight hairs stood on the back of his neck. They floated as though they were manipulated by a swaying breeze. He used the kennel to stabilize himself. A swarm of frigid air bit at his exposed flesh. He twisted his torso and drank in a familiar entity that stood several feet taller than him.

One feminine face carved from marble stared down at Vasilij, her chin pointed and long, while two others assumed the remaining planes of her oblong head. She carried two torches in two hands, their colors the same copper hue as the sconces that lined the hallway. Four remaining arms, each appearing fragile yet absurd in their length, spread out and gracefully arched toward the stunned Vasilij.

Flesh-against-flesh, his face stung from her icy touch as she navigated her fingers around his square jaw, strong jowls, flat forehead, and through his matching crops of hair planted on either side of his bald spot.

He didn't realize his eyes were squeezed shut and he very much wished for the witch to disappear whenever he found the courage to open them.

She spoke in his native tongue and a waterfall of resonance washed over him in dull euphoria. Her energetic voice layered in an ensemble of three tones. Each of them combined to create a dissonant chord. "Why are you afraid? You and Anna are free to leave this place."

His voice shrank. He felt like a mouse staring up at a panther. "W-we are?"

"Of course. Regardless of how, my ritual was completed. Congratulations! As a reward, you two are bound to me as familiars for having witnessed this ceremony, just as several generations of those tied to this building have become."

Vasilij's voice seeped. "No. I'm just on vacation. I'm on vacation. Me, a familiar? No, no. I'm on vacation."

"This is *good* news, don't you see? This situation benefits both of us. I have lost one, but I have gained two."

"What—what do you mean by..."

"You will meet before me once a year, in this very location, to ensure the ceremony is maintained. Three bodies, posed as dogs—suitable substitutions for the real thing, since this building has been repurposed. Having eliminated my last familiar, it is now your responsibility. It is, rather, an obligation, Vasilij."

Her cold voice speaking his name nearly deafened him.

Vasilij clutched either crop of hair. His eyes watered and searched the deity's unshifting expression for empathy. His gaze, though hard and focused, returned nothing.

"You have no choice but to agree."

It moved a fraction of an inch closer, and he dropped to the ground, clawed backwards, and kicked away from the entity until he found his shoulder lying against the bathroom door. Vasilij repeatedly punched at the wood and pulled himself up, using the frigid doorknob to do so. "Anna! We need to go!" he shouted in his native tongue. "Please, come outside. Anna! *Anna!* Please, please! You were right! We need to leave!"

The crackling of bones and the slithering of flesh. The woman's second face spun into position, and he marveled at its similarity to the hound that stood by her side. When she opened her mouth to speak, a bellow crumpled him back to the ground. Vasilij shouted in short verses as fear tackled his nervous system. Swaths of dark cloth heaved during her graceful movement forward.

He looked up at the titan and lamented her horrible image. Her four free arms were cocked outwards, her fingers rigid and pointed. "This is meant to be a reward." she delicately claimed, her voice rising slightly. "A bounty claimed by few. The masters of this building are obedient, just as I hoped you would've been."

"No, n-no. No! Anna? Anna—*please!*"

The three-faced woman glided forward in a single, swift motion. Her third face spun to face him: a serpentine mask with two pinpoint holes for a nose.

"*Please!*" Vasilij tried the door handle once again. The brass bracket loosened from the wood as adrenaline pumped through his veins. "Oh, God. We need to leave! Please, please!"

The deity curiously observed the human's tantrum while he failed to hail a response from Anna. She paused in benevolence. "You are unwilling? Then, another deal will be made." An internal timer drained to zero, and both torches dropped to the ground, extinguishing upon impact. "I am nothing if not flexible."

"She's not listening to me," a heavy tremolo oscillated his voice. "She's not listening to me. Open the door, Anna. Please let me in! Let me inside!" Vasilij's words dribbled out and repeated on end until all six of the woman's vascular arms shot toward him.

Her long nails perforated his torso, tore away his shirt, and tossed chunks of flesh and muscle along with each wild movement. Machinery—her arms were like machinery. Organic, but unnatural, with each puncture perfectly synced to an internal metronome. Before Vasilij could wriggle free from the shallow attacks, one of her many hands gripped his jaw and forced him back into position. Their eyes were locked into a tandem staring contest, a sick game he couldn't hope to win. The face spun to that of a horse, then back to the hound, before winding to the serpent with, at some point, dizzyingly impossible speed. The entity's head became a spinning top of horrible expressions.

These many hands were straightened into perfect weapons. Her elbows cocked back and plunged forward with each attempt digging a fraction deeper. This ever-so gradual mining of his chest cavity was performed with such surgical precision, Vasilij couldn't feel the titan extract his ribs. One by one they were bent and snapped in diminishing halves until her fingers met the warmth of his organs. *This is pain,* he decided. *This is actual pain.*

His cries subdued until he became silent, then obedient, then dead.

11

*"Something is happening." Jenny's mother said
calmly and without moving her lips. "Embody awareness."*

*

There was enough sense left in Jenny Novak's aching
skull for her to feel hesitant when standing at the front desk
of a visibly decaying bed-and-breakfast somewhere deep
within a country she should've never visited.

Sabiha tapped her lifelessly dull fingernails against
the keys of a counting machine. The woman looked up to the
occupant of room nine with pink, swollen eyes, and a
glistening upper lip. "Eighty."

Jenny's jaw tensed. "What? No, I'm leaving now. This
place is lovely, but I don't need to stay another night."

She sniffed, wholly disinterested in creating eye
contact. A polaroid of her, Romeo, and a handsome,
dark-haired young boy stole her attention. Its corners were
folded, the color faded as though it'd been bleached by
overexposure.

Jenny felt fairly certain the photo hadn't been pinned
to the corkboard when she arrived.

"You already sleep here for two days."

"No, that's not... Really?" She checked the date on
her dying phone and dropped her jaw. "Are you kidding me?
I..."

The deep lines of webbing from Sabiha's lips wriggled. "It... Happens occasionally." She screwed on a smile when Jenny frowned at her. "You come back next year? Please do."

"I..."

Sabiha pressed on with a trembling bottom lip. Her eyes bore into the guest like an automatic drill. "Next year, same time as this time. Yes? A—a good price for you if you do."

Jenny hesitated to exchange the small stack of euros even though Sabiha's trembling left hand desperately hung mid-air. "Sorry, I didn't even—I didn't realize I was out for so long. I have to call my grandfather, tell him I..." she shook her head, winced, and grazed the back of her head. Jenny bit down on her knuckle until the pain subsided and watched the micro-movements of Sabiha's textured face flicker and tense.

"Eighty. Please."

"Right. Yeah." Jenny sighed and handed over the crisp bills. Her eyes drank in Sabiha's defeated appearance as she counted the amount. Red eyes, a tight jaw, and unkempt strands of hair looped in untraceable directions. Sadness seeped into Jenny's heart. "Hey, Sabiha?"

The woman looked up from the cash, her expression wooden.

"Are you feeling okay?"

In an explosion of emotion, the woman cursed in Slovenian and turned away from Jenny. The paper bills floated to the desk and to the floor.

Sabiha covered her mouth to stifle her wails. She stomped through the lobby before disappearing into the great hall located directly under the stretch of rooms located one floor above them.

Sucking on her teeth, Jenny widened her eyes and reached down for her bag. "Alrighty, then."

As if called to action, Romeo rushed to the scene. He hovered at the entrance to the great hall and crossed his arms.

"Hey, Romeo," Jenny nodded to him with a bit of surprise cast on her face. "Is everything okay?"

His nostrils widened, but his lips were kept tight and thin. He kept his steely eyes focused on her. They watched each other for a moment, and Jenny offered a toothy smile from across the room. The man's focus divided unevenly between the great hall and his Australian guest.

Jenny considered her potential review:
two-out-of-five stars: the first day was great! staff was friendly and helpful, owners were a delight, but i somehow slept for two days and they didn't even bother to wake me up even though so they charged me for two days even though i only wanted to stay for one day and when i asked the owners about it their tense demeanors no longer created a welcoming or comfortable environment so all i wanted to do was get the fuck out before they poisoned my breakfast or something.

In the communal lobby area, an old man with a knot on his head and an elderly woman with a thousand wrinkles were chatting between themselves.

"Nothing at all?" the woman asked with a cute tilt of the head. Her soft eyes scrolled from the top of her companion's head down to his polished shoes.

"I wouldn't say *nothing*, but I desperately wish there was *more*."

"Would you like to play what you do have, then?"

He laughed a genuine, perfect, and floaty chuckle—one that didn't hold a modicum of ego. Jenny felt as though she hadn't heard laughter in years. "I'm not even sure what your name is."

"Rene," she said in her obvious German accent. Before he knew it, he kissed her hand. "And you are?"

"Martin," the man replied. "Like the guitar."

"Martin-Like-The-Guitar. I would love to hear what you have."

Jenny hovered at the edge of the lobby with her bag in hand and a smile neatly tucked on her face. The old man grunted as he relieved his acoustic guitar from its case and placed it over his right knee. He pursed his lips and blew away any dust from the neck. "I don't take as good care of her as I should."

Rene leaned back into the chair that boasted a sewn, golden tableau of dog faces. "That's okay, dear." She reached across to the side table where a detailed ceramic mug waited for her. Martin's thumb traveled from the fattest string to the thinnest with an attuned ear. Nodding in approval, he strummed the first chord as soon as the cup reached Rene's lips.

A coquettish smile formed behind the mug's lip. Jenny could no longer mistake the soft longing in her eyes as she watched the American man play her a personal concert.

"Featherless dove,

133

Flightless and yet above,

A pitch-white place,

Three mirrors showing each face."

Martin slid just out of key when he ascended to the higher register of his voice.

"The forest waits,

Every step falls into place,

A tapestry,

Above us, shields us from grace."

He sustained a diminished minor chord and matched the ringing with a soft hum. "Now, I swear I had written the perfect bridge—lyrics and all!—but I can't remember a damn thing. I think I even switched out the first two lines with something else... That's me growing old, sleeping through alarms and forgetting things. With that said, that's all I can offer you, madame."

"Well, it's simply not enough," she replied with a wink. His cheeks blushed, and he looked to his guitar for emotional support.

Jenny approached the two with a small hop. "You're not old, sir," she said while providing a comforting smile. Her appearance startled him at first, but it felt to her as though Rene expected her arrival.

"I saw you admiring him from across the room." In a whisper that almost acted as parentheticals, "*I saw him first!*" Martin blushed at the comment and rested his hand over his face to shield his emotions from the two strangers. Then, in a normal voice, she asked Jenny, "Wasn't it a lovely song, dear?"

"Definitely!" Jenny grinned and Martin looked away with a shake of the head. Her voice lowered, and her tone tightened. "I'd just like to let you know that I also slept through my alarm. So, yeah! Turns out, you're not that old after all."

Martin nodded, sizing up the unfamiliar face. "Miss Rene, as well. Curious, isn't it? Maybe this place knew we needed a good night's rest."

The three shared light, rattling laughter. Romeo's gaze intensified and scathed her right cheek. She faced him, forced a smile, and excused herself from Rene and Martin. They nodded and settled back into a comfortable, low-volume conversation as if Jenny had never even been there.

"Hey, so—my head is killing me. D'you think I can get some of your 'world famous' coffee? To-go, if that's possible?"

Romeo lifted his chin, swelled his chest, and said during his exhale, "One moment." He scratched his eye and turned to the kitchen.

A high-pitched whine droned in Jenny's right ear. Rays from the youthful sun burrowed through the fogged windows and assaulted her senses. Doom swallowed her. Standing in the building felt like she had been tied to a stake and was close to being consumed by flames. No longer able to bear the sensation, she fled through the front door before Romeo could return.

The door creaked shut behind her.

Jenny's sensitive eyes paved the path between her feet and the short flight of crooked stairs. She very much cherished the fact that her feet eventually reunited with the earth. Stretching her legs felt like walking for the first time. Her eyes traveled to a thicket of trees, an outcropping that made up an entire system of woods. The trickling of a nearby stream excited her heart and helped to dredge a half-buried memory from the shallow pool of her consciousness.

An animal of some kind, she blinked. *Was it raining, or was it just foggy outside?*

When she focused too hard on it, the image disappeared.

A strident voice of a young woman sang in hysterical despair nearby. Jenny's eyes locked onto the leg of another guest. A maroon stain ate through her jeans and ruined the expensive-looking fabric. The guest shouted into her cell phone: "You piece of *fucking* shit! I don't know if you're having a laugh or what but leaving me in this *shithole* is *not* my idea of a goddamned *joke*, Christopher!"

She pressed the receiver to her chest and wailed a pent-up sob before returning to berating Christopher's voice mail. "I was literally attacked in the middle of the night and now you're gone. Did you do this to me, you joke of a man? Answer the phone right now, or I swear to Christ I'll call Auntie Jane. Pick up, you idiot! Pick up! Pick up, pick up, pick *up*, *pick up*, *p-pick*..."

While the scene was addictive as watching a car crash, it wasn't her place to leer. After all, only four months ago did Jenny herself outside of a Starbucks screaming at her then boyfriend to pack up his belongings before she returned home. She remembered the strangled whispers each barista passed between one another.

Deciding to feign disinterest, Jenny blinked away the remainder of her sudden ice pick headache and trudged through the loose gravel of the parking lot.

A red-headed woman rounded behind a rusted truck and shouldered her away. The pain—which had been much more than she could fathom from such a small bump—caused her to abandon her backpack to the mulch. "Jesus shit!" Jenny shouted and reached for her right arm. It stung when she applied any pressure to her right shoulder. "Damn it."

"Oh, so sorry," the woman said in a saccharine German accent. "I-I can be such a klutz sometimes. I'm cursed, you see, to always be in the wrong place at the wrong time."

Jenny creased her brow and absorbed the woman's outfit: a stylish green-gray trench coat, slips, leggings, and a pair of dainty square glasses hanging off the bridge of her nose. A shimmering red bob flounced when she tilted her head. Two identical lacerations crossed either wrist, half-hidden by the sleeves of her coat. "No, it's okay. It's... I'm sorry. Do we...?"

The woman blinked twice, shrugged her thin shoulders, and said, "Know each other? I've been in plenty of commercials, but none of them you've seen. Not unless you've visited Germany in the nineties."

"No, I haven't," Jenny ventured a weak laugh. Muted disappointment caked the woman's face—a clay mask that cracked and peeled with every additional movement. "And not unless you've ever visited Sydney." The stranger shook her head.

"Did you enjoy your stay? What room were you in?"

Jenny mustered a thoughtful response after babbling an incoherent string of syllables. "Uh, nine. And, I mean," she started with a tense rise of the shoulders. "It really is beautiful here. I just wish I could've explored the grounds a little more, but I'm a whole day behind... Somehow."

"Well, I know I'll be back next year," she smiled without sustaining direct eye contact. "Maybe we'll see each other again. Sorry again for bumping into you! I'll hope to have learned how to embody a little more awareness by then." Jenny's heart sizzled. "Goodbye, room nine."

Jenny tracked the woman as she re-entered the bed-and-breakfast. Romeo planted like a statue in the doorway. Both of his massive hands gripped what she supposed was her mug of coffee.

An undefined guilt, one that hemorrhaged in waves, remained even after the door closed.

There was enough sense left in Jenny Novak's throbbing skull for her to leave the threshold of a visibly decaying bed-and-breakfast somewhere deep within a country that didn't want her and finally drive to the arms of a loving grandfather who did.

Acknowledgements

Kristen Schmidt *(for her continued support and unconditional love)*

Rachel Oestreich *(for her talents as a developmental editor)*

Andrew Rivard *(for his continued support and very conditional love)*

Tim Hacker *(for being my number one fan)*

Cindy Thai *(for being a phenomenal artist and always offering support)*

The Whole Rabbit Podcast *(for both inspiring and supplying an incredibly supportive community)*

About The Author

Cody Ray George is an Atlanta-based author born and raised in Central Florida. He is influenced by the likes of Hideo Kojima, David Lynch, and Charlie Kaufman.

He grew up in a haunted house, in a haunted town, in a haunted state. Having been entrenched in the paranormal from a young age, it was only natural for him to turn out this way.